Once Upon A Goth Dog Solstice

A Once Upon A Story Holiday MM Romance

R.L. Merrill

ONCE UPON A GOTH DOG SOLSTICE

From the author of the award-winning novel *You Can Do Magic: Carnival of Mysteries* and Publisher's Weekly BookLife quarterfinalist *Earthquake Ethan* comes a heartwarming holiday tale of found family and sacrifice. Two wildly opposite veterans connect over a shared love of art, rescue dogs, and a very special foster child.

Air Force veteran Doug Cross has made a fresh start in the San Francisco Bay Area with a room on an urban farm, a thriving cyber security business, and a new spot in a goth punk band. He's a helper by nature, so when his housemate mentions needing to raise funds for her dog rescue, he puts his artistic skills to work making goth-inspired dog accessories to sell at the Treasure Island craft fair. He also lends a helping hand to the artist in the next booth, and the two have a potential meet-cute...that quickly fizzles, leaving Doug wondering why his charming personality failed to make a new friend.

Single foster dad Luther Sorenson is a disabled Marine veteran who is struggling to keep his family afloat—and himself literally on his feet. He's selling his wood paintings at the fair when his body decides to quit on him, and he is forced to ask for help from the goth guy next door. It could have been humiliating, but Doug makes it easy, and Luther can't stop thinking about him in between markets. Not his superb makeup skills, nor the way he rocks a utilikilt either.

The two begin a tentative courtship, but as the seasons change and their responsibilities pile up, they'll have to learn to strategize if they're going to successfully navigate life with an adorable foster daughter, a grumpy rescue dog, and their crafty endeavors.

Once Upon A Goth Dog Solstice is a part of the multi-author series Once Upon a Holiday Story. Each book can be read as a standalone and in any order. What links these books together is The Hook's Book Nook Traveling Library, a library on wheels owned by two old ladies in love.

Storelli
*I miss the Skittles and Jolt Cola days. You are a gift and an
inspiration. Much love.*

PART ONE
SPRING EQUINOX

ONE

L^{uther}

Luther Sorenson's daily morning routine involved pain, determination, and a lot of old man noises. He needed to work up the courage to straighten his legs, swing them over the side of the bed, and plant his feet on the floor if he was going to get through the day. If he got that far, then he'd push himself to shuffle to his yoga mat and go through the excruciating process of completing the PT exercises he'd been doing since the accident three years ago. This routine meant the difference between a day of crippling pain or manageable dull aches that would allow him to complete his tasks with minimal distraction.

He'd never be in the shape he was in before the accident, but at least he could walk, could still move. He was fortunate. His VA benefits provided some assistance for nontraditional treatments, which was good, because none of the surgical options were guaranteed to work, and he was looking at a lifetime of managing debilitating pain. He struggled, but he'd do whatever was necessary in order to continue with his most important purpose...

"I had a bad dream."

Eight-year-old Mila Saavedra stood in the doorway of Luther's room with a stuffed dinosaur hanging limply from one hand. Her other hand was pressed against her stomach.

Luther turned over and sat on his yoga mat with his arm out, gesturing for her to come closer. The brief seconds she hesitated to move toward the mat gutted him. Once she settled on a course of action, she approached him, not front on but coming around the mat to stand nearer his side.

"What happened in your dream?"

Mila sat cross-legged and folded her hands in her lap with Terry D'actyl against her body. It was still tough to get her to make eye contact, but Luther knew better than to push that issue. It hadn't worked with him as a young man, and he was determined not to make the same mistakes as the foster parents *he'd* lived with.

"I went to school and no one was there to greet us. I went to my classroom and no one was there. No one came to take us to lunch. I sat at my desk all day, and no one came. And at the end of the day..." She ducked her head, and Luther heard the shaky breath she took in.

"At the end of the day, I come to get you."

She shook her head.

Luther let out a breath. As much as he hated to revisit his past, Mila's social worker, Miss Vanessa, told him from the start that building rapport with his foster daughter would likely require him to find ways to connect with her around their shared experiences.

The whole reason he'd become a foster parent was to help other kids avoid having *those kinds* of shared experiences.

"I used to have dreams like that, too."

She lifted her head long enough to look at him from under her thick bangs, and then she looked at his feet. "What did you do?"

Luther definitely didn't want to get into all of the negative ways he'd coped as a kid. That was in the past. But he could tell her about the ways he coped with life now.

"When I have bad dreams now, I exercise, or I go work in my studio. Those are things that make me feel better." He let out a breath and thought how much he wished he could spend the day with Mila, but he'd signed on to work the art market on Treasure Island one weekend a month, and today was his first day. He'd gone over and parked his trailer in his spot the previous night, so he could scope the place out. He'd been a little nervous about registering to become a vendor, but once he'd stepped out of his truck and breathed in the San Francisco Bay breeze, he'd allowed himself the briefest moment of peace. The view of the San Francisco Bay at sunset was breathtaking, the weather was forecast to be mild, and he'd finally have a chance to see what—if any—kind of money he could make selling his wood paintings.

It had been his sister's idea for him to try selling the art he usually reserved as gifts for his closest friends. Violet helped him research vendor opportunities, got him registered for this one, and helped him get everything set up to run a business. She volunteered to stay with Mila on the days he'd be at the fair. If he hadn't already known how incredible his sister was, well...now he knew she was an absolute gift.

"I like to fix things," Mila said quietly. She reached over and tentatively touched a tiny hole in the hem of his sweatpants. "My tummy feels better when things are all right."

Luther's own stomach clenched at her words. "Mine does, too. What do you think would make things all right this morning?"

She glanced at him under her bangs. "I wish I could sew," she nearly whispered. "I could fix your pants."

Luther wanted to reach out and take her hand, but Miss Vanessa had suggested he wait for her to engage with him when *she* was ready. She'd been with him for six months now, and they'd made huge progress, but he was determined to do everything right so she could have a chance to heal. He wanted to make things safe for her, give her a place to find herself.

"These old things?" He tugged at the cuff and showed her the inside. She gasped at the barely attached threads. "Don't you worry about these. I've had them since before I was in the Marines." There was a hitch in his voice as he mentioned his previous calling. He cleared his throat. "If you tried to sew these holes, the material would likely disintegrate in your fingers. Auntie Violet will be up soon. She's an expert at sewing."

That got him a timid smile. "Would she teach me?"

"I'm sure she will. She taught me."

Her eyes bugged out. "You know how to sew?"

Luther let out an exaggerated sigh. "Marines know everything, remember?"

She groaned and squeezed Terry tight. Then she turned him around and pointed to a seam on the critter's back that was barely hanging on. "Do you think I can fix this?"

Poor Terry had been through it. Luther had gently tried to replace him, but every morning he'd find Mila's arms wrapped around the beat-up pterodactyl. He was the only toy she'd been able to bring with her when Miss Vanessa took her from her unsafe situation, and Luther knew the two of them had seen some shit together.

"I do. Now," Luther said, looking at where she still had a hand on her stomach. "What can we do to fix your tummy?"

She tilted her head as though it was a difficult decision, but Luther knew her answer.

"Pancakes?"

"As if it would be anything else. Come on," he said, knowing that cutting his exercise time short would bite him in the ass later, but he was determined to give the world to this little girl, no matter the price he paid.

He managed to push himself up off the floor without cursing and he took it slow as he straightened his back, stretching his arms above his head.

Mila needed no prompting. She was out the door and humming on her way to the kitchen. Luther used his phone to start her playlist on the Echo in the kitchen and she squealed in delight, singing along to Etta James. His girls loved jazz, and since he'd give them just about anything they wanted, this special playlist was all they listened to.

Luther had just served Mila's pancakes with bananas when Violet joined them in the kitchen. She was a night nurse in the ER and was usually getting home at this time. Today she was dressed in workout clothes and hadn't bothered with her usual elaborate makeup and hair.

"Swapped shifts so I'd be bright-eyed and bushy-tailed for Miss Thing this morning." She stuck her chin out and waited for Luther to kiss her cheek before he slid a plate in front of her. "How are you this morning, Miss Mee-la-la?"

Mila giggled. "Good now. Auntie Violet? Can you teach me how to sew?"

Luther's stomach finally unclenched as Violet turned and smiled at him.

"I've been dying for you to ask! Let's eat, and then we'll get started, little mama."

Mila lifted her shoulders and grinned. She made eye contact with Luther for the briefest moment, but long enough for him to see the joy in her gaze.

This morning might have started off rough, but things had come around.

He had to keep the faith that they would continue to.

He took a lightning-fast shower, dressed, and packed up his painting kit in case he didn't have customers, so he'd have something to do.

"I'll be home around seven," he said, cringing at how long the day would be. "Mila, make sure you listen to Auntie Violet, and if you're both good, maybe I'll bring home treats."

He rarely kept sweets in the house, they were too much of a temptation for him, but he'd noticed that the spot next to his was a mini-donut vendor.

"Yes, sir," Mila said, but instead of the soft-spoken voice full of fear she'd used when he first brought her to his house, her voice was bright, almost happy.

"I'll be *such* a good girl," Violet said, batting her long fake eyelashes at him. Violet had been placed in the boys' home where Luther had been living when they were both freshmen in high school. On her first day there, Luther had stepped in when other kids started talking shit about her makeup. The foster system hadn't known what to do with a trans kid back then, so Luther made it his job to educate the others on how to treat her. It hadn't taken long for them to respect her, and she took care of them all at one point or another when the group home staff was too busy to do so. They'd bonded over that and many more experiences, and when they'd both turned eighteen, they'd gotten a place together.

She was the only family he had, until he'd decided it was time for him to give back and become a foster parent himself, and she agreed to support him however she could. Luther and Violet against the world. It was that way then, and it always would be.

He bent to kiss Violet's cheek again, and then he stood next to Mila's chair with his fist out. She'd typically gaze at it warily and then bump it with hers. This morning, she grabbed it with both hands, pulled it to her cheek, cuddling it for a second before she let it go to shove more pancakes into her mouth.

Slow and steady wins the race, soldier.

The drive from Hayward this early on a Saturday morning only took about twenty-five minutes. Luther parked his F-150 in the vendor parking lot in a handicapped spot, which he hated to do. He rarely used his placard, but his spot was quite a hike from the lot. Luckily, he'd been able leave his trailer at the back of his space so he didn't have to cart all of his wares in. He carried a backpack with his money box and the lunch he'd thrown together this morning, along with two large water bottles. Staying hydrated was key.

It took him an hour to set up his canopy and hang the mesh panels he'd built to display his paintings. He had to take frequent breaks to stretch his back. He'd tried to use the lightest materials possible and found two lightweight aluminum tables for the inside of the booth that he covered with simple black tablecloths. He hoped his art would speak for itself.

He was just out the framed QR code signs that Violet had made for him, but when he opened his cash box, he realized the credit card reader he'd bought wasn't inside.

This was a problem. He knew people didn't carry cash much these days, and though Violet assured him the QR codes for the payment apps would do the work for him, he'd spent a lot of time figuring out the credit card reader.

He looked around his booth and sighed. He'd hoped to sell at least half of his paintings. Would this derail his plan?

What might derail his *focus* was the loud laughter and music playing from the booth next to his. *Goth Dog Rescue?* He put his hands on his hips and peered through the mesh in between paintings to discover it was exactly what the sign said.

Dog collars and dog clothes. Dog treats. Dog bowls. All with a funny skull on them that had a mohawk. Huh. Then he spotted a large banner with pictures of dogs with handlers, a dog sitting in an airplane, and a QR code for donations to Goth Dog Rescue.

Luther swallowed back a swell of emotion.

It had been a long time since he'd been around a dog. Three years, to be exact.

A man and a woman chatted excitedly and sang along to... The Ramones?...as they set up the booth, which was way more elaborate than Luther's. And when the guy turned around, Luther gasped.

The guy looked as if he'd be way more at home in a club than outdoors on a sunny day. With pale face makeup, elaborate black eye liner with glitter, black lipstick, and hair styled in a faux mohawk, he definitely fit the name and the artwork of their booth. His shirt was from a punk band, and his arms were covered with brightly colored tattoos Luther couldn't make out from the distance between them.

They were toned arms, though, and they were attached to a guy who definitely looked like he spent at least some time at the gym. Luther sighed. It had been a long time since he'd seen the inside of a gym. Even longer than the last time he'd spent with a dog. He missed that life, some days more than others. His life now was focused on providing stability for Mila and for himself, maintaining what little mobility he had and keeping extra pounds off that would exacerbate his condition, rather than packing on the muscle and pushing himself to build endurance for when he was deployed—

He suddenly remembered there was one more place he could look for the card reader. He hurried toward his cargo trailer, which he'd bought used from a Marine pal before his injury, to haul his motorcycle. He was glad to have it now, though the motorcycle was long gone. He could eventually kit it out and make a mobile sales trailer if he wanted. He climbed through the barn doors in the back and attempted to step over the wagon he'd packed just in case he needed to carry his things far and his leg decided...nah.

Not today, soldier.

Two

D^{oug}

Doug stepped back and took in the glory of the Goth Dog Rescue booth.

He wished he'd had time to airbrush a sign for the top of the pop-up canopy, but for now, they'd just use the one Dinah had been using that had the name spelled out in a basic font, and then had an illustrated dog face on the side. At least the dog had a mohawk.

"We're going to make a killing today," Dinah said, hip-bumping Doug. "I cannot thank you enough for coming onboard."

Doug smiled at her and shrugged. "No thanks necessary. You're letting me stay with you and giving me an outlet for my art, which keeps me out of trouble, honestly."

Dinah Shaw was Doug's cousin's girlfriend and she ran Goth Dog Rescue out of her family's urban farm. The rescue had been running on donations up 'til now, with a little help from the homemade dog treats Dinah made. Thankfully, Bay Area folks were happy to support the cause, but shortly after moving in with the Shaws, Doug had had a drunken revelation while partying with his cousins Marianne and Matt, and Matt's husband Zack, at the Shaws' farm.

Goth Dog Accessories.

He was a whiz with a sewing machine, an airbrush, a riveter, and plenty of other tools, as well as having a knack for turning leftover stuff into works of art, which could be sold for additional funds to go to the rescue. They were starting out with collars, airbrushed bodysuits, and wall signs with the new logo he'd designed, plus he'd brought his equipment so he could personalize all of the items. He had loads of ideas, but today was their test run.

"I bet we sell out by noon," Dinah said, looking at her watch. "You got this for a minute? I'm going to go check on Cecily."

Dinah's sister raised goats on the farm. She used the milk they produced to make soaps and body lotions. She had her own booth at today's fair, as well as selling her goods weekly at the local farmer's market. Dinah would be going between the booths today to help out with sales, which was fine. Doug was comfortable with the sales point and the pitches about their goods and the dog rescue.

He was taking one last look at their set-up when he heard a crash and muffled swearing from the booth next door to theirs.

"Need a hand?" he called out, moving quickly. The booth had large mesh panels affixed to the sides of a canopy, as well as tables in a U-shape to display intricate nature paintings on pieces of wood of all sizes. The owner of the booth had a silver cargo trailer at the back of his space, and that seemed to be where the muffled cursing was coming from. Doug peeked around the side and was greeted by a back covered in plaid flannel.

"Hey," he said, his voice low to hopefully not spook the guy, but that failed.

The man stood and tried to turn, swore again, smacked his head, and stumbled backward.

"Whoa." Doug caught the larger man's weight as he fell backward out of the trailer, which thankfully wasn't too high off the ground. He steadied the man as he got his feet under him. "You all right, man?"

"What are you doing back here?"

The voice didn't quite match the appearance, which was serving grumpy lumberjack or maybe curmudgeonly stuck-in-the-'90s grunge fan. No, the man's voice was soft-spoken, despite his gruff expression. He did not appear thankful or welcoming.

Doug pulled his hands back as the man angrily stepped out of his grasp, but then the guy crumbled a bit, his hand going to his lower back, and he leaned against the trailer while letting out a long breath.

"I didn't mean to startle you," Doug said, trying to let his shiny personality warm up this interaction. "I recognized someone speaking my language and thought I'd offer assistance."

The guy turned without straightening to his full height, which appeared to be a couple of inches taller than Doug's five-nine.

"English?" The guy lifted his lip à la Billy Idol. He had a dark blond buzz cut that looked as if it was a few weeks past a haircut and a matching beard that could use some taming, but his hazel-green eyes were sharp, as if he was accustomed to being on alert. Former military maybe? Doug glanced at the trailer again and...*ah*. USMC sticker.

"Ah, no, well, I meant Frustrated Male. That is, if male is

how you identify. I shouldn't assume." Doug gave a nervous laugh. He usually didn't have trouble winning over new folks, but this one seemed to have a fortress up meant to keep cheeriness away. "I'm already set up, so I thought I'd see if you needed any help?"

The guy winced, and then managed to stand upright. "I'm fine. I...I was looking for something. It's a tight fit in that trailer."

"Sure, for someone your size." Doug knew he shouldn't be taking the opportunity to admire the tight fit of the man's pants. He really should be a better human than this, *but here we are*. "Would you like me to look?" It was better to be helpful than to ogle, right?

The guy cursed again and planted his hands on his hips. "It's the thing for the credit cards. Forget it. They're about to open the gates. I'll get along without it."

Doug felt bad for the guy. "If you have Venmo, they have a tap function now. I could show you."

"I'm good." The guy stood and moved to the rear of his booth, where he could see all the customers but not necessarily chat with them.

"Okay. Is this your first event? It's my first time. My roommate has been doing this for a while, but I'm new." *Big smile, big smile. How can he resist?* And not even from a queer perspective. Doug was just the kind of guy who made everyone smile. Well, unless you were of the goth-hating variety, what with his shaggy, dyed-black hair and his daily use of makeup. Today he'd dressed in tight black pants with zippers up and down the legs, lime green Dr. Martens, and a Misfits tee with the arms cut low on the sides. "I'm so glad we got a spot for this market. It's gorgeous here."

Doug had a habit of turning on the verbal hose and blasting folks with it when he first met them, and this guy was apparently his latest victim.

But the man didn't respond. He stood there staring at Doug, bewildered, until the first group of customers started filtering into their aisle.

"Welp, if you need anything," Doug said, realizing he'd definitely overdone it, backing up toward his booth. "And have a great day...?"

The guy nodded at him with a frown, missing Doug's attempt at asking his name, and then he started adjusting his paintings. Doug checked out the ones hanging nearest the wall separating their booths as he passed by, and he was suddenly transfixed.

The guy had taken pieces of fresh-cut wood with the bark still on the outside, and he'd painted lovely forest scenes with flowers and sunshine, mushrooms and moonlight...there were even some fairy houses hidden in the shadows of giant redwoods. Oh, Doug would definitely be buying one before the end of the day. There was an almost whimsical quality to his work, as if it would appeal to nature lovers and children alike.

Doug turned to say something, but the guy was pounding his thumbs into his phone, his forehead creased with an almost caricaturish depth from his scowl. Doug glanced around once more to see if the guy had a name on his booth, but there was nothing.

"Dougie! You've got customers!"

Dinah was bouncing on her toes as two women stood at their designated pay station, their arms loaded with collars, bodysuits, and dog bowls. They each held leashes with black and white King Charles Cavaliers attached. Such cute pups. Doug had always been a big animal lover, and living with the Shaw sisters had been paradise. Between the farm animals and the foster dogs, there was always a critter to cuddle with, something he desperately needed in his life. Who could survive without cuddles?

"Awesome. Would you like any of that personalized?"

"Oh my goodness, yes, please! Could you? For Mugsy and Mojo?"

Doug grinned at the names. "Absolutely." He went around the table to the station he'd set up for personalizing. It was behind their booth, so he didn't get paint anywhere it shouldn't be. "We can put them aside to dry, and you can come back before you leave the market to pick them up."

They were thrilled. Doug got to work with his airbrush, adding their names in script to the two bodysuits. Then he did the collars and the bowls. He was so busy, he didn't notice that the neighbor was standing behind his booth, watching him.

He removed his mask and started to say something, but then his neighbor had a customer. Before he knew it, Doug had spent the two hours personalizing items for their customers.

"Phew," Dinah said as she took a drink of her home-brewed peach tea. "It's only eleven forty-five and we've already sold out of bodysuits and bowls."

Doug stood to look at their inventory, and he wrinkled his nose. "That sucks. I mean, I'm glad we sold a lot, but I hate to see empty shelves. Hey, if you don't mind staying out there, let me get out those doggie t-shirts I ordered and I'll start airbrushing them. They'll dry quick and we can hang those up. Hopefully those will be popular too."

Dinah looked down the aisle to see that Cecily had two customers. "Let me just check with Cecily. Maybe we should think about combining our booths so I can help both of you."

"Or we could clone you," Doug said with a shrug. "I swear, I'll have way more stock next time. At least we know the stuff sells."

Dinah squeezed his shoulder. "You are a gift, Doug. With this money, we can afford for Marianne to do more rescue flights, and we won't have to max out the credit cards to keep the fosters fed, not to mention the vet bills. That last litter of pups we took in all had respiratory infections, and that cost a pretty penny in medication."

"You guys are doing such great work. I'm happy to contribute whatever I can. The fruits of my labor are yours."

"At least there are some perks to the job. You get to pet cute pups all day," she said, as Doug's gaze drifted once more to their sullen neighbor.

He didn't interact with the customers unless they specifically asked him questions, but he seemed to have a steady stream of folks admiring his work. Doug started picturing ways to highlight the gorgeous paintings. Weave green moss into the mesh he'd used to hang the paintings; add some fairy lights, especially since it was darker in the back corners, which made it difficult to see the intricate details in his paintings. Doug wanted to offer suggestions, but he doubted they would be welcome.

It took him another two hours to spray paint the dog shirts he'd brought, and by the time he had them all hung up, the rest of his inventory was sold out, and Dinah's treats were gone as well. She'd gone over to help Cecily, who was also just about out of soaps and lotions. This was *wild*. Doug was wondering how much money they'd made versus their costs—

"Oh, rats. I'm so sorry!"

Doug turned to look into his neighbor's booth in time to see that a woman had bumped the mesh and one of the panels had pulled away from the canopy, which caused a few of the smaller paintings to fall onto the ground. The man was trying to hold up the mesh and bend down to pick up the paintings at the same time. The woman was older and distracted, and she wandered away from the booth to leave the owner to deal with her clumsy mess.

"How can I help?" He reached for the mesh. The guy made what Doug thought might be an appreciative grunt? If that was a thing. But then he bent down to pick up the paintings, and he cried out, his hand going to his lower back again as he caught himself on a table with his forearm. Sweat broke out on his forehead.

"Oh man, leave those. I'll grab them." Doug managed to get the mesh fastened quickly, and he went to the guy's side. "Let me help you," he said softly.

He could tell his neighbor didn't want to accept his help, but he dropped his left hand into Doug's extended right one, clasped it hard, and leaned heavily on Doug to climb back to his feet.

"Can you get me to the trailer? Please?"

That soft voice attempted to hide the pain this man was in, and Doug wanted to give him his dignity however he could. He helped the man to the back of his booth and over to the doors of the trailer. The man used his keys to open the padlock while leaning on Doug, and then he opened the doors. He turned and took Doug's other arm so he could lower himself to a sitting position on the trailer's ledge.

"What can I get you? Ice? Water? Some anti-inflammatories?"

The guy was taking shallow breaths. He pointed to a water bottle on the back table of his booth. Doug reached for it and handed it over. The guy took a sip and then a few deep breaths.

"You okay for a second? Let me go grab those paintings."

Doug went to step away, but the guy kept hold of his arm for a minute.

"Thank you," he said, locking Doug in place with those sharp eyes.

"Sure, man." Doug went to pick up the paintings. He brushed them off with a napkin he'd had in his pocket to hopefully get the dust off without messing up the man's work. He readjusted the ones that were knocked askew and was about to return to his fallen neighbor when another customer came up to the table with two paintings.

"Oh, um…" He turned to his wounded neighbor, who handed him his phone.

"Do you mind? I just need a minute."

Doug knew it had taken him a lot to ask for help. "Sure, how would you like to pay?"

The woman held out a credit card. "I only have a credit card. I don't use apps."

Doug smiled, determined to make this sale go through. She had about three hundred dollars' worth of art there. "Give me a second?"

He went and knelt beside the proprietor. "Hey, I know you said you couldn't find your card reader," he said quietly. "But would you like me to set up tap pay for you through your app?"

"I don't know what that means."

Doug nodded. "It'll allow you to take credit cards, and this lady has two of your big paintings."

"Okay. Can you—" He winced and took another sharp breath. "Can you show me?"

"Absolutely." He had the guy open his app, and then Doug took over, walking him through the easy steps. He pulled out his own wallet, removed his Visa, and did a test payment for a dollar, and it went through with a flourish of sparkles on the guy's phone.

Doug's phone immediately sent him a notification. *Payment to Luther Sorenson.*

Niiiice. Intelligence acquired.

"All set. Let me handle this for you."

"Thank you."

The guy's cheeks were rosy above his beard. The color would have made Doug happy, except that it seemed more from exertion than from a bashful flush.

Doug checked the woman out, wrapped her wood paintings carefully, and placed them in one of the paper bags his neighbor had on the table.

She waved to Doug as she left, thankfully heading next door where, hopefully, she'd spend a little more cash for the puppers.

"Here," Doug said, handing the handsome man his phone, grateful to see he was breathing a little easier. "Anything else I can do for you?"

"I...no, thank you. You saved my ass."

"Saving your ass was my absolute pleasure," Doug said with a play bow. "How's the...is it your back? Injured in the Corps?"

Luther sat up a little straighter. "How'd you—" When Doug pointed to the sticker on his trailer, he nodded. "Oh. Yeah."

"Damn. Sorry to hear." He stood at attention. "Senior Airman Doug Cross, at your service." He held out a hand, this time to shake like mens.

"Air Force, huh?" Luther accepted the handshake and looked Doug up and down. "You out?"

"Hells yeah. I was a reluctant enlistee. Daddy's expectations. Did six and split. Was recruited by a civilian contractor for my..." He wiggled his fingers above an imaginary keyboard and clicked his tongue against his teeth. "I'm so over the military-industrial complex. Now I pick and choose my clients, I make art and music, and leave the house looking like this." He gestured to himself with a laugh.

Somewhere in that little diatribe, Luther must have taken offense to something he'd said. His curious expression closed off and his nostrils flared.

"Right. Well, thank you." He stood and gave Doug a look like their conversation was over.

"Right." For some reason, Doug hated that he was being

dismissed. He'd thought maybe they could at least talk shop a little, maybe swap arty-farty hacks, but no. Luther stood from his trailer, took a deep breath, and went back to reorganizing his paintings to fill in the gaps. "Well, let me know if you want any help tearing down—"

"I'm good," Luther said without turning around.

"Right." *Dougie, you need to learn when to shut up.* "Your work is phenomenal," he said, as he was about to leave.

He almost missed the quiet, "Yours, too."

Okay, okay, so maybe he hadn't won this encounter...but perhaps next month?

Doug looked at his phone and realized the market was closed now. A quick gander at their booth let him know that they'd sold most of everything they'd brought.

"Hot patootie, bless my soul," he said, as he high-fived Dinah.

She responded by singing the rest of the line from the *Rocky Horror* song. "Are you ready for the tally?"

A shiver ran through him. "Hit me."

She looked down at her phone, tapped the screen, and then held it out.

"That's not including the payments to the other apps. This is just credit cards."

They'd made over six thousand dollars.

They both screamed simultaneously and hugged each other while they hopped up and down in a circle.

"I bet we made another few hundred on the other apps," she said quietly, realizing their carrying on had attracted notice. "And we had to turn people away because we sold out!"

"And imagine how much we could do if we bring puppers!"

They'd talked about having a few of the rescue pups in a pen to lure folks in, but Dinah thought they should bring a couple of Goth Dog volunteers if they were going to do that.

"I bet we could get Nell to come at the very least." Nell was Doug's cousin Matt's daughter and an active volunteer in the Goth Dog community.

They continued to plot as they tore down their booth and packed everything into the back of Dinah's black minivan. The back windows were covered with '80s new wave band stickers and a huge Goth Dog decal in the middle. It didn't take long before they were done. Doug kept trying to catch a glimpse of Luther, but he was nowhere to be seen. He was happy to see that he'd sold a large amount of the paintings he'd brought, especially the small ones. He'd meant to pick one up. Damn. Next time?

He spotted Luther returning with a bag from the mini donut truck and thought, ah...the guy has a sweet tooth. Maybe he could whip up a little peace offering for their next visit. He still didn't know what he'd said to cause the abrupt termination of their conversation. If Luther had been injured in the Marines, he most likely shared the sentiment that the majority of veterans had when dealing with the VA: No one gave a shit about broken soldiers, and they sure as hell weren't going to help you start a new life.

Doug regularly volunteered with and donated to veterans' organizations. He'd been grateful to get out relatively unscathed and with a skill set that made him a hot commodity. It was now his choice whether or not he wanted to utilize those skills, and right now, he'd chosen to do what made him happy. Which reminded him...

"Hey, do you mind if I help you unload tomorrow morning? I've got a gig in Berkeley tonight."

She clapped her hands. "Yes, you do, and we're all coming to watch!"

Part of the allure of coming to the Bay Area was to be near his cousins while he made art, but he was also interested in the music scene, and he'd auditioned recently for the East Bay

Goth Punks. They'd been grateful to find a vocalist who could also play guitar and keys. Their sets consisted of '80s punk and new wave tunes, all super fun, and they hoped to start writing originals.

Doug was hoping he could encourage them to branch out a bit, once they were used to him, but for now he was just stoked to have musicians to jam with. He hadn't been in a band since high school. The Air Force hadn't given him the space, and, well, during the time he'd spent with the civilian contractor, he'd been practically sequestered. He'd made a shitload of money and had no life. It was time to refill the creative well.

He sighed and smiled. He'd landed in a great situation here. He was finally getting to spend time with Marianne and her brother Matt's family, he had a fantastic place to stay with the best housemates he'd ever had, and he was able to work on his art and music while taking on a minimum number of cybersecurity clients. He was living the life he'd dreamed of back in high school while towing the Dwight Cross line: God, Air Force, and country. Nowhere in there was there room for individuality and happiness.

"Then let's get to it!"

He gave one last lingering glance in Luther's direction as they drove Dinah's minivan down the aisle, and he winced when he saw the painstakingly slow way Luther was moving as he packed up his gear. Doug should have offered to help again, he should have insisted...but no. He hadn't made a friend that day, which surprisingly overshadowed his success a bit.

And wasn't that an epic bummer.

Part Two
Summer Solstice

Summer Solstice

THREE

L uther

"I hate that you two had to get up so early on a Saturday."

Luther tapped his thumbs on the top of the steering wheel of his truck as he drove through the toll plaza for the Bay Bridge. He snuck glances over at Violet, who had barely gotten home from a harrowing Friday night ER shift, showered, thrown her hair up, and put on sunglasses. Mila, still in her pajamas, was cuddling Terry D'actyl in her booster seat in the rear cab of the truck and bouncing her feet along to the sassy "I'd Rather Be Burned a Witch" by Eartha Kitt, who was Violet's idol.

"After the state you came home in last time, there's no way I'm letting you set up by yourself."

"Gilly and Stu are deployed, or I would have asked them. They helped me take down last time. And Tex is..."

"Unreliable. Your jughead buddies can't drag their asses

out of bed this early on a weekend, so here we are. We'll get you set up, and then Miss Mee-la-la and I will be back at the end of the day to pack you up."

"Jarheads." Luther gave her a bashful smile. He had a couple of buddies he'd served with who lived in the East Bay, but they worked hard during the week and partied hard on weekends. Luther wasn't about that life anymore. Once again, Violet had come through for him.

"Whatever." She raised an eyebrow at him and crossed her legs, folding her hands over her knee.

"Why we can't stay all day with you?" Mila asked from the back.

Luther's smile turned joyful. His foster daughter had made great progress in the past three months. It had started with sewing lessons and the triumphant repair of Terry D'actyl, followed by repairs to every hole in Luther's clothes—including a pair of his boxers—before he let her know his clothes were just fine as they were.

Now that she was finished with school for the summer, they'd been spending a lot of time together. She liked to work on her new skills in Luther's studio—the converted garage of the house he shared with Violet—while he completed paintings for the upcoming show. Once she'd mastered basic stitches, she learned to make a simple vest for Terry to wear, how to sew patches on clothes, and this week she'd started a simple embroidery pattern on a pair of her pants.

Luther had taught her that skill. Embroidery kits had kept him from going bonkers during downtime while deployed. He could only put Bunk through his training so many hours of the day. Even his beloved furry partner-in-crime had needed downtime.

He'd thought more about his fallen comrade since sharing space with the Goth Dog folks at his first Treasure Island market. When he'd mentioned the dog rescue to Violet, Big

Ears had overheard "foster dogs," and she'd had so many questions.

"You mean there are dogs like me? They get foster parents too?"

The one that broke Luther's heart?

"But where do they go when their foster time is up?"

Mila had been distraught when, in one of their meetings with Miss Vanessa, the social worker had mentioned that Mila could stay in foster care until she was eighteen, and then she would transition to independent living. Luther had thought that was a complicated concept for an eight-year-old to understand, and sure enough, a week later, Mila had made a couple of comments about when she had to leave Luther's house. She'd had tummy aches for a week straight. He'd been ready to take her to the doctor when she'd finally asked where she would go when she couldn't stay with him anymore.

"Mila, you will be my family as long as you want to be, even after you turn eighteen. Just like Violet. When we left our foster home, we stayed together. You can stay as long as you want. This is your home."

That had settled her, but then she asked, "Would you ever want another foster child?"

Luther thought about that. "I don't know. Would you?"

Mila had shrugged, then she frowned. "Would you ever have a foster *dog*?"

And that had stumped him. He'd always loved dogs, and when given the opportunity to join the elite working dog handler training as a Marine, he'd jumped at the chance. He'd never had a dog of his own, and the opportunity to bond with one made being deployed a little easier.

He hadn't realized how much it would break him to lose a K-9 partner. Could he bring another dog into his life after Bunker?

Luther blew out a breath and ignored the stinging in his

sinuses as he took the exit off the Bay Bridge for Treasure Island and wound his way around the hill to the site of the market. He'd come to believe the views from this place were the most incredible in the whole Bay Area. From the Oakland Port to the Berkeley Hills, and from the San Francisco skyline to the breathtaking bridges, there was beauty and strength in every direction. You could watch sailboats and windsurfers and watch giant cargo ships passing under the bridge. There had been a military presence here for decades, but between community events like the market, new housing, and a Job Corps center for youth trying to make a life for themselves, the island was reclaiming its identity.

Luther had always loved living in the East Bay, despite his troubled youth. Now he had a different perspective on life here, and he was grateful for the opportunities this area presented.

He pulled up to the vendor lot and put the truck in park. "I can manage it alone," Luther said quietly to Violet, trying to give her an out.

She lowered her glasses and looked down her nose at him. "Miss Mee-la-la, bring your jacket. It might be chilly out there this early."

Mila unbuckled herself and grabbed her puffy jacket.

"I owe you, sis," Luther whispered.

"You know better," she said with a smile. "Let's go, team."

Luther led them over to his booth and was relieved to find that the Goth Dog folks weren't setting up yet. He didn't want an embarrassing repeat of having to be rescued by the confounding Senior Airman Doug.

His tummy gave a little flutter at the thought of Doug's strong arms coming to his aid not once, not twice, but three times at the last market. Funny how he and Mila had the same nervous ailment. He'd been humiliated, but then Doug had made it so easy to accept the help. And he'd been *so* damned helpful. When he'd fixed a fallen panel, when he'd accepted payment from a customer...when he'd smiled.

Face it.

Airman Doug was mouthwateringly gorgeous.

Until he'd made it clear how he felt about the military and those who willingly served.

What a crushing disappointment.

Unlike Doug's wish to cut and run as soon as possible, Luther had planned to make the Marines his career. The Corps had been his life. He loved the purpose the Corps gave him, and he loved his friends. He'd always believed in helping people and had been willing to make sacrifices for his country.

He'd just never allowed himself to dwell on what that sacrifice would entail. After twelve years of service, he received a medical discharge. It became clear that eight months of rehab hadn't fixed him enough to continue to serve. He couldn't run, much less complete the physical requirements to remain, and there hadn't been any paper-pushing opportunities for him, either.

Thank you for your service, Lance Corporal Sorenson. Good luck.

The two years since had seen the development of a bulging disk, bouts of sciatica, and terrible osteoarthritis. He was now thirty-five years old and moved like he was eighty. What would he be like at fifty? Seventy? His disability payments were enough to pay his share of the mortgage on the house he and Violet had purchased together, thank God, and his basic needs. The stipend he received for taking in Mila was plenty to cover her basics, but he wanted more for them. He wanted a savings for emergencies, he wanted to take her on a vacation.

The painting had been something he picked up to keep from going stir crazy. He'd been artistic as a kid, and as a teenager he'd discovered he had a knack for painting. He was self-taught, and after the accident, he'd had nothing but time to improve. Between YouTube videos and practice, he was pleased with his schtick. Violet and Mila had assured him others would be too.

"You can't just fill up our house with your art," Violet had said. "Other people deserve to enjoy it too."

Selling his art was the next step, and hopefully he'd make a decent amount of money to cover the supplies as well as start socking money away for Mila.

The art was one thing, but he was starting to think about getting a part-time job in the fall, something he could do when Mila was at school. Miss Vanessa said she'd help him when he was ready. He *needed* to be ready.

"This is you? Oh, look at that. Goth Dog Rescue. I've seen their flyers around downtown Hayward."

Luther frowned as hard as he could and clenched his jaw, hoping Violet would cease and desist.

"Rescue? Are these the people who put dogs in foster homes?" Mila asked. She stood staring at the sign with her fists on her hips, which would have carried more weight, but she had Encanto pajama pants on and, much to Luther's chagrin, her werewolf-feet slippers for shoes. In his haste to get out of the house, he hadn't reminded her to change. Now he'd have to figure out how to clean fake fur. Mila loved those goofy things, and he'd bend over backwards to make sure she was surrounded by things that made her happy.

"It sure looks like it," Violet said, ignoring Luther's jaw clenching. "And they've got a pen set up. I wonder if they're going to have dogs here today?"

Luther shrugged. The Goth Dog booth had been on a different aisle the past two markets, and while he'd been glad to avoid more awkward interactions with Doug, he'd also missed the entertainment his neighbors had provided.

Doug never quit moving that day they'd met. He'd created masterpieces with his airbrush, helped customers, and danced around the booth singing along to whatever vaguely familiar music was playing.

Luther had always been a very visual person, and he hadn't stopped thinking of the way Doug moved as if he had a live wire running through him, the way he casually wore intricately applied makeup on a sunny Saturday, and the way he smiled with so much joy anytime he spoke to, well, anyone. The whole time Luther was being his usual serious self, Doug had acted as if he were in his favorite place in the world doing the things he loved most.

Luther envied that type of enthusiasm. He used to have some. That was before his life was irrevocably changed on a dark night in a foreign desert.

Imagine his surprise when he heard singing and gravel crunching beneath the wheels of a cart, and his heart gave a little hiccup.

"Howdy, neighbor," Doug said, giving him a wave as he approached. "I see you brought reinforcements."

Luther opened his mouth to speak when Violet blocked his path and held out her hand.

"I have you to thank for helping my brother before?"

Luther saw the briefest glimpse of confusion before Doug's black-lipsticked smile spread wide. They got that a lot, with Violet being a gorgeous Black woman and Luther being an ordinary white boy with dark blond hair and pale hazel-green eyes.

"No need to thank me," he said, gazing mischievously over her shoulder to Luther. "Pleasure was all mine."

Now, why did Luther's face feel hot all of a sudden?

"And who might you be?" Doug asked, crouching down to Mila's level.

She tilted her head slightly, and Luther waited to see how she'd react.

"Mila," she finally said. "I like your makeup."

"Thank you," he said, giving her a big smile. "I like your pterodactyl. What a cool vest!"

She looked down and tugged on the vest to make it lay smoothly. "I made it with Auntie Violet."

Doug glanced up at Violet. "No kidding. I make vests too. Want to see?" He looked to Luther for permission, and he nodded, knowing full well he could see them the entire time.

As Doug led Mila to his booth next door, Violet came to stand next to Luther.

"You conveniently left out of your description that this man is all kinds of fine. I mean, look at those legs. They're works of art."

Luther had tried very hard to ignore the fact that Doug was wearing a black utility kilt today, topped off by a sleeveless black tee with silver studs along the collarbones. He had on a little less eye makeup today, but he'd drawn some intricate swirls with some sort of rainbow glitter along the tops of his cheekbones. He also wore rainbow socks over the tops of his Dr. Martens.

"Feel free to go over there, then."

Violet hip bumped Luther. "I'm here to help you set up," she said, frowning at him. "And I'm not exactly dressed for flirting purposes. You, on the other hand," she said, her gaze traveling up and down Luther's body. "You know I love that color on you. I think you're more his flavor."

Luther had grabbed his last clean, decent t-shirt today, which happened to be a faded red one that clung tightly to his chest. He'd stuck it at the bottom of the drawer for a reason. He hated anything that showed off the fact that he was no longer in excellent condition.

"Yeah, well." What else could he say? Sure, he was intrigued by the guy, but he'd gotten a stick up his ass when Doug mentioned he hadn't wanted to be in the military.

Luther needed to get over himself, and he knew it. The

Marines had chewed him up and spit him out—he knew that, too—but they'd also given him a purpose and confidence when he was a young, scared kid with nowhere to go. He'd made good friends, learned important skills, saw more of the world than he'd ever thought possible—even if a lot of it was places he never would have gone intentionally—and it had given him four years with Bunk.

As if he'd manifested them into existence, Doug's partner came walking up with four dogs on leashes. They weren't quite pulling her, but it was a chaotic sight. Doug hurried over and opened the pen door in time for her to herd them in.

"Mila," he called out. Luther was unsure how she'd react to the dogs, but she merely stood there and watched with interest while Doug introduced them all to her.

"That's Joey, Marky, Dee Dee, and Tommy," he said, pointing to each of the youngish mutts in the pen. "Like The Ramones. They're all from the same litter. My friend Dinah here rescued them," he said, gesturing to the woman with him. She was wearing a black halter and red high-waisted pants with black polka dots and buttons up the front, with bright red lipstick. These two made quite a pair. "Dinah talks to animal shelters all over the state, and when they get too full, they ask her to take some of their dogs because she's really good at finding the perfect homes for them." He was bent over with his hands on his knees, talking to her on her level. It was unexpected. And hot.

Mila's eyes widened. "She's a social worker?"

Doug stood up straight and gave me a surprised expression. "I hadn't thought of it that way," he said with a shrug toward me. "But I guess that's a good description. Hey, Dinah? Are you a doggie social worker?"

Dinah turned from where she was hanging dog collars on a hook and smiled at Mila. "I suppose I am. I like taking in strays," she said, winking at Doug.

He rolled his eyes at her. "Strays. Ha ha."

Interesting.

Luther wondered if Doug would have questions for him later. Luther *wanted* Doug to have questions. He wanted to talk to him more; he could only hope that he'd worked up enough courage over the past two months of thinking about him to hold a pleasant conversation.

At first, he'd thought no, he had his hands full with Mila, and besides, what could they possibly have in common?

Then he realized, *duh,* they were both visual artists. He hadn't had another artist friend before unless you counted Violet, who was art personified. Besides makeup and sewing, she designed clothes and interior spaces. Occasionally she also picked up discarded pieces of furniture, turned them into something wonderful and unique, and then sold them online in her Etsy store.

And after a conversation with a fellow disabled veteran at physical therapy, he realized he hadn't been real fair to Doug. Everyone had their reasons for enlisting, as well as leaving the service. It was the fact that they'd served that made them all a part of something bigger, and whether you had a good or a bad experience, it was still a *shared* experience.

So when Luther saw the map for this weekend's market and saw that Goth Dog Rescue would be next to him once again, on the end of their aisle, he decided it was a sign that he should apologize, maybe try again to make a connection.

It appeared all he'd needed to do was have his daughter with him to get Doug's attention.

"Let's get this set up and I'll get her out of here so you can, you know, sell stuff." Violet had obviously caught on to Luther's distraction.

"Copy that."

They went about hanging up this month's paintings. Luther had focused on summer themes and he'd mixed it up.

He not only had his usual wood cuttings, but he'd also found some wooden trays and boxes at local thrift stores he'd thought he could do something with. Violet had helped him sand them down so he could turn them into new pieces of art that could spruce up any space.

He'd even been inspired to make something for Doug. It was corny, true, but now he needed to work up the courage to present it to him. It was the least he could do for the kind way Doug had helped him last time. Of course, that was why. No other reason.

When all of the panels were hung, the paintings displayed, and the tables covered with the new trinkets Luther had made for this event, Violet raised an eyebrow at him.

"You be careful today. Rest. Stretch. Drink your water."

"Yes, ma'am," Luther said, standing at attention. He could do that now. Two months ago, he'd started an anti-inflammatory diet, a Hail Mary endeavor to try to get some relief, and it was helping. He'd noticed he had a tad more stamina and flexibility. The pain wasn't quite as intense. It wasn't a lot of help, but it was enough to give him some relief. It had improved his mood, as well.

Perhaps it had also opened his eyes to the possibility that he'd been an ass, and that maybe he could use a friend.

"Come on, Miss Mee-la-la," Violet called. "Time to go."

Mila pulled Terry to her chest and stared at Luther from her spot next to the dog pen. She hadn't tried to touch the dogs, but she'd been watching them closely.

Whoa. Luther wasn't sure he was ready to even think about adding more chaos to their chaos, especially with his physical limitations. Puppies needed chasing. They were loads of work.

Memories of his first days with Bunk took his breath away. The German Shepherd had already been through basic training, but he was a young dog and full of energy. Even when they weren't training, Bunker needed stimulation. He was the most enthusiastic dog he'd come across in the service. His devotion to Luther had made their time together while deployed much more tolerable. He'd had something to focus on other than the hairy situations they dealt with daily as part of the force deployed to protect the US Embassy in Kabul and the airport, so Afghans with ties to the US could escape the Taliban.

Bunk hadn't made it home from that mission.

Luther shuddered and let out a breath as his chest started to get tight, and he felt a twinge in his lower back.

"Luther?" Violet said, putting a hand on his arm. "You okay?"

He nodded and gestured for Mila to come to him. She took the smallest, slowest steps possible away from the dog pen until she was out of the Goth Dog Rescue booth, and then she quickened her pace until she was standing in front of him, her gaze on Terry.

"You like the puppies?" he asked her.

She nodded.

Luther looked at Violet, and then bent down as best he could to get on Mila's level.

"Would you like Auntie Violet to bring you back a little early so you can see them again?"

Her gaze finally met his, and she nodded vigorously. He didn't quite get a smile, but that was okay. She had come so far in the past couple of months. He had faith that they would continue growing closer.

A dog would be a great way to bond with her. He reached out and squeezed her shoulder. Maybe he needed to deal with his own ghosts for her sake.

"I think we can do that," Violet said, squeezing Mila's other shoulder. "We'll see you later, LuLu."

"Bye, Daddy."

Luther smiled at Mila and touched his heart. That was a recent change as well, one that let him know she was finally warming up to him and the idea that they were family.

He waved with his left hand as they walked away, his right still over his very full heart.

"She's awesome," Doug said, coming to stand beside him. "How old is she?"

"Eight. She's my foster daughter."

Luther noticed that Doug's blue eyes brightened, and the lines beside his eyes deepened as he smiled.

"That's so cool. My cousin and his husband fostered and then adopted their daughter Nell. She's coming to help out with the dogs in a bit. That's...really great, man."

Luther realized this would be the best opportunity to make his presentation. Ugh, that sounded so corny in his mind.

"I...you have a second? I brought something for you." His palms grew clammy as he waited for Doug to answer.

"Sure, yeah."

"Great." Luther turned for the back of his booth and opened a large plastic bin. He bent at the knees and lifted out the wine crate. He was careful to stand straight before he turned and put the black lacquered wooden box on the end of the table.

Doug's eyes bugged out. "What is this?"

And here was where Luther grew self-conscious.

"I, uh, I noticed last time that, uh...your airbrush machine...you carried it in a bag. I thought, maybe this might be sturdier. I could make a cover for it if... Here."

He turned it around and Doug covered his mouth with a hand.

"Oh my God. Luther! That is... I can't believe you did that!"

Luther had the idea for the painting when he was going

through a stack of vinyl at the last flea market he'd gone to, looking for boxes. He'd noticed the RCA logo and thought it would be perfect. He'd painted it just as it appeared on their albums, but he'd added a black mohawk to the dog and on the large horn of the Victrola, he'd painted their Goth Dog logo.

Doug lifted his gaze to Luther's with a questioning expression, and Luther wished it wasn't quite so warm already. He was sweating and worried he'd have sweat stains soon. Had to be the heat. He hadn't totally lost his ability to keep a cool head in a tense situation. Had he?

FOUR

D oug

Luther's creation was so damned thoughtful that Doug felt silly sharing his peace offering.

"This is the perfect size, and you're right, that compressor is heavy. Last month, I caught the tote bag on something and nearly lost my whole unit when the canvas ripped. This is incredible." The box looked about the size of a wine crate and had handles cut into the wood. The painting looked identical to the RCA logo. "Thank you so much, Luther. What a kind gift."

Luther's cheeks turned pink above his beard, which was cut shorter than last time. He'd had a haircut too. Something had happened to him, something good. He seemed to be in much better spirits than he had three months ago.

Doug had been kicking himself since that day, wondering what he might have said to offend the guy. The past two markets he'd baked his heart out to have a sweet treat for the sad man, and both times they'd been assigned to different spots on the other side of the vast market, and they'd been so busy, he hadn't had time to sneak away from the booth to see if he could find him. He'd told himself he'd try one more time, *this* time, and if he didn't run across the wounded Marine, he'd give up and accept that they weren't meant to be friendly.

"It's funny that you brought this. I made you something, too."

Luther planted his hands on his hips and his eyebrows rose. His face was very tan, with smooth skin, his hair the color of wet sand streaked with flecks of pyrite, his beard darker. Doug hadn't seen him smile yet, not a real smile, and he hoped his offering would do the trick.

Doug held up a finger, trotting around the corner of their adjoining booths.

"Hey, can you set up that spinning rack for me? I want to get the rest of the collars hung on it. I think it's really helped give us more space." Dinah was trying to get the hooks into the pegboard so they could hang up all of the little doggie t-shirts he'd made.

Doug moved close to her and spoke in her ear. "Luther brought us a gift. I'm going to give him the muffins I baked."

Dinah's eyes flared. "Go go go," she whispered, shooing him away. She grinned at him and went back to work.

He'd spent hours lamenting to Dinah and his cousin about his previous conversation with Luther. Finally, Marianne had smacked him upside the head.

"Not everyone who leaves the service wants to leave it behind, Airman Egghead. Some veterans hang on to their service as a way to avoid having regrets about their lives, and to others, it was an accomplishment they're proud of. That's how I felt about it. It was the situation that forced me to retire that I hated. I have lots of good memories."

Whatever the case, Doug intended to hand Luther the baked goods, his protein-packed power muffins, and give him a big fat apology.

He carried the reusable carry-out container over and handed it to Luther.

"Here. I baked you apology muffins. They've got extra protein so they'll help you make it through the day. I'm sorry."

Luther held them in his hands, staring at the container, and without looking up, he said, "Why?"

"Why am I sorry? Because I obviously said something that offended you last time, and it's been bothering me since."

Luther wrinkled his nose and shook his head. "You didn't. I was in a bad place that day and acted like a jerk. Why did you bake for me?"

Doug tugged on his kilt and rolled onto the sides of his feet.

"Because I wanted to do something nice, and I noticed you buying some donuts before you left last time. I deduced that maybe sweets were the way to your heart."

Overshare. *C'mon, Doug. You don't even know if this guy—*

"I *do* like sweets," he said, his lip twitching. "I don't let myself have them usually." He opened the container, pulled one out, and took a bite out of it. His eyelids fell closed, and a crease appeared between his brows. If Doug wasn't mistaken, that was a look of bliss.

"Good, huh?" he said, breaking the quiet between them.

Luther grinned with his lips closed and swallowed his bite. "You put chocolate chips in them."

"I did."

"They're still warm," Luther said, tilting his head to the side.

"I wanted them to be fresh. I got up early and made them this morning."

"That was very thoughtful of *you*."

Doug shifted his weight, gave a little bow, and smiled. He wished they weren't about to be inundated with customers because he thought maybe, just maybe, they'd made a break-through.

Luther maintained eye contact as he finished the muffin, licking his finger before he closed the lid. "I bought those donuts for my daughter and my sister."

"Uh-huh. I'll let you decide if you're going to share your muffins." He turned to walk back to his booth, but he watched Luther as he went, running his fingers over the edge of the panels displaying Luther's paintings.

"Don't forget your box," he said. He put his container down and picked up the box.

"Right, thank you." Doug went to take it from him and their fingers tangled in the handles he'd cut into the side of the box. They both chuckled, and after a minute of attempting to shift the weight to Doug, Luther got his fingers free. But he didn't let go right away. He ran the fingers of his right hand over Doug's again.

"Enjoy."

Doug turned to go back to his booth and caught Dinah's eye. He mouthed, "Oh my God!" just as Luther called out to him. He turned around, nearly knocking a display over with the box. "Yeah?"

"Like the kilt."

And Luther smiled. Not quite a full-toothed affair, but Doug was mesmerized nonetheless. At least he had it together enough to make a comeback.

"I'm glad."

He spun on his heel, which caused the pleats to lift enough to show a little more leg. Doug had been given a second chance—and he wasn't above a little exhibitionism.

"You did that on purpose," Dinah teased as he set the box

down next to his painting station. "This is gorgeous. He did this?"

"Be still my heart," Doug said with a sigh. "Guess I'm not on his bad list after all."

Dinah snorted. "Even if you were, you wouldn't be for long. It's impossible to be upset with you for long."

He pulled her in for a side hug and kissed her hair. "You say such things. Thank goodness my cousin snagged you."

"I know, right?"

Business was double what they did last month. The warmer weather, the puppies, and Doug's new merchandise—he'd gone a little tie-dye hog wild, and he'd made matching dog and human shirt combos for summer with their logo on them— had their inventory flying off the hangers. They were sold out by two in the afternoon.

He'd been so busy he hadn't even had a chance to check on Luther. Oh, be real, he'd wanted another opportunity to speak to the man. He'd started to come up with scenarios where maybe they could hang out when they weren't working. How would that work, though, with his daughter? And did he have another job?

He snuck a peek and noticed that Luther's tables were nearly empty of the new wooden boxes he'd brought and many of his paintings were gone as well, leaving space for him to watch the man through the mesh panel.

As if he'd heard Doug's thoughts, he lifted his head after handing a customer their bag and lifted one corner of his lips in an amused expression. His gaze seemed mischievous, like maybe he, too, was wondering what they could get up to together.

Doug wasn't sure if the need to fan himself was from the heat, or the looks he'd exchanged with Luther.

He sat down in his chair and sighed. He was grateful it was officially summer, but he hadn't really been able to celebrate the changing of the season from spring to summer just yet.

In years past, he'd made a point to find a solstice celebration. One year he'd been in the UK, so he'd gone to Stonehenge with thousands of others seeking to commune with the spirits. All he'd gotten was sunburnt on a rare sunny day. Last year he'd been in France and celebrated the Basque festival of Saint-Jean-de-Luz, which was a little mix of pagan and Catholic and lots of fun. That had been a great trip, but he'd been a little lonely wandering around the Spanish city of Bilbao by himself, both before and after.

The purpose of the summer solstice was to reflect and prepare for the next part of your journey, but Doug didn't want to look ahead. He'd been living in the now since leaving the civilian contractor's employment, so all that reflection he was supposed to be doing made him twitchy. He didn't want to plan for a future, didn't want to settle down. He wanted to enjoy this time with his family and his housemates on the farm, so that's what he was doing.

A little fun with the hot painter in the next booth sounded pretty awesome too.

"I can't believe it," Dinah said, flopping into her chair. "We made enough today to cover the cost of building the new kennels at the farm." There were a few dogs who hadn't gotten any interest and Dinah wanted to be able to take them out of the pens she'd built for them in the small barn on the Shaw property and give them room to run. She and Doug had drawn up plans for some long runs with a shelter at one end, so the pups could run between the barn and a new enclosure, where they could set up agility courses and a play yard in the shade for the pups. Doug loved being part of such a great program and was thrilled that his contributions would allow Dinah to rescue more dogs.

"I'm already thinking of what I can make for next month," he said, rubbing his hands together.

"Nell got seven applications for the four pups today, and several folks asked about other dogs we have available. All of our rescue literature is wiped out. I think it was a good move, bringing the dogs. Thankfully, these four are pretty mellow for puppies."

Nell joined them. "I'm happy to come back next month. It might be tough when I'm back in school in the fall, but I don't mind giving y'all a hand. Any excuse to play with pups, I'm there."

Doug high-fived her. "You rock."

The angle of his chair allowed him to watch Luther as he moved around his space. He seemed to be a little stiffer than he'd been that morning, but he didn't have that pained expression that made Doug so worried last time.

"Hey, Doug? Can you show me how you did your glitter makeup? It looks so cool. I can't believe it still looks fresh after working all day."

He looked around at their empty space and shrugged. "I can show you now. Want me to do yours?"

She clapped her hands and Dinah laughed. "You two have fun. I'm going to grab some food and check on Cecily. I hope her soaps aren't melting in this heat."

The temps had risen after lunch and were now in the high seventies, mitigated by the breeze off the Bay, but Cecily's booth was in the sun.

"We got this. No worries."

He pulled his chair over next to Nell's beside the puppy pen. He pulled his makeup kit out of his bag and held it up. "I come prepared. I had a gig last night."

"Again? Man, y'all been playing every weekend, huh?" Her eyes lit up. "Oh hi!"

Doug turned around to see who Nell was talking to, and

he grinned when he saw Luther's sister, now with her hair in an updo and her makeup done, dressed in a halter dress and wedge sandals. And she had Luther's daughter with her. Violet waved at him with a smile before she gave Mila a little push toward the puppy pen. Luther joined Violet at the front of his booth, giving her a hug.

"Welcome back," Doug said to Mila with a wave. He set his makeup out on Dinah's chair. "We were just getting ready to do a makeup tutorial. Want to be my model?"

Mila was dressed in shorts and a top that had bow ties on top of her shoulders. Her thick brown hair was long and straight in the back, and cut blunt across her forehead, which obscured her facial expressions a bit.

"I don't know. Daddy?"

She turned around to call to Luther. Doug noticed the man's face soften as he gazed at her.

"Yes, Mila?"

"Can I have a makeup tutor?"

Violet smiled wide at Doug and elbowed Luther with a nod.

"Sure, honey, as long as Doug isn't too busy."

Doug gestured around their booth. "Plenty of time."

Luther nodded and pressed his lips together before Violet stole his attention away.

"Here," Nell said, standing and letting Mila take her chair. "I want to watch him do it. I'm Nell, by the way."

Mila gave a brief glance at Luther, who was barely ten feet away, and then looked back at Nell. "Pleased to meet you. I'm Mila."

Nell shook her little hand, and then Mila turned to look at Doug with wide eyes.

"First of all, do you mind if I put your hair up so it doesn't get in the makeup?"

She nodded and folded her hands in her lap as she studied his makeup kit.

Doug felt around in his bag and found two hair clips. He used them to pull the two sides of her hair back. She was so tiny sitting before him in the chair, he didn't want to frighten her. He glanced over his shoulder and saw that Luther and Violet were talking and watching him. Violet was grinning and Luther looked...curious.

"Nell asked me to show her how I did these rainbow glitter designs. Is it all right if I show her on your face?"

She sat up taller and nodded in rapid movements.

"Great, here we go."

Doug started to draw, and Nell and Mila both watched his movements. He had a couple of great eyeshadow palettes with the perfect colors to do the swirls, and a clear glitter paint to seal it all in.

"You were telling me about the band," Nell said.

"Oh, yeah. It's fun, but between the gigs and practice, the time I'm putting in making the inventory for these markets, plus my cybersecurity clients, I haven't really had the chance to hit many of my Bay Area bucket list items."

"You'll have to make time," Nell said. "What's on your list?"

"Oh, you know," he said, "Mila, I want you to raise your eyebrows and close your eyelids, okay?"

She did exactly as he asked, so good in fact, her little jaw was tight with the effort, the tendons in her neck popping out.

"You can relax a little," he said, chuckling. "I don't know. I want to visit a few of the local haunts, you know? Winchester Mystery House, Alcatraz, the Presidio. Some cool, out-of-the-way places. Don't get me wrong, I'm having a great time. I just want more, you know?"

He dabbed at his palette and when he looked up, they were both looking at him curiously.

He had her eyeliner done and was about to draw some of the rainbow lines coming off the swoop of black at the corner of her eyes.

"I don't know. I'm just…antsy I guess. I left home so long ago I don't even remember what it feels like to have a home. Everything's been so temporary," he started. "I do want to settle down eventually, but where, I have no idea. And what would that even look like? I can't stay at the farm forever, and my cousins aren't going to want me hanging around."

"Doug, you know that's not true. My dads love that you're here. Auntie Marianne, too."

"I love it too, but…I don't know. When I left the Air Force and went to work for the private contractor, I felt like my life was slipping away without me really living it, you know? I want to do things on my terms, not have any regrets or wish-I-could-have moments."

"I know I want to travel," Nell said. "But this will always be my home base. I want to be near my family. I've only had them for eight years. It's not enough time."

"That's right," Doug said. "I tend to forget you were adopted as a teenager sometimes because you guys are so tight."

"I was lucky," Nell said, leaning down so she could see Doug's work closer. "A lot of kids from my group home stayed there 'til they were eighteen and were then out on their own."

Doug blew out a breath. "I can't imagine. Although, there were times when I wanted to be anywhere other than home. My father's expectations made my life miserable. As much as I didn't want to enlist in the Air Force, I couldn't wait to get out from under his rule."

Mila opened her eyes wide and looked between them.

"That looks so fancy, Miss Mee-la-la," Violet said as she joined them. "Your makeup game is strong, Doug."

"Thanks," he said to her. "Just have the final glitter to add. You ready?"

Mila shut her eyes and raised her eyebrows, tensing her jaw so much it made her head shake.

"You can relax your jaw, sweetie. Okay. It's going to feel a little cold, so hang in there."

"Okay," she said.

"I get it," Nell said. "Grandpa Mason isn't like that, but I've heard him grumble about his brother from time to time. It's amazing how men in the same family can be so different."

"Tell me about it," Violet said. "Women, too. My auntie fought to have me live with her, but my mother, her sister, refused. Then my mother kicked me out of the house when I was fourteen. I went to school and told them I had no place to go and boom. Group home. Thrown to the wolves. Thank the Lord for Luther, my protector."

Doug took that information in and tried not to appear shocked. So Luther had been a foster kid, too? His heart melted in his chest. What an honorable man...a thoughtful, kind, and talented man, who'd been through several kinds of hell and was obviously determined not to let this little girl go through what he did.

Doug wanted to know more. He wanted to *know* this man intimately. In his desire to experience life to the fullest, he had dated plenty of men and women, and met plenty of interesting people, but he'd yet to find someone with depth. Or at least, he hadn't connected with someone on a deep level.

"That's cool you're still close," Nell said. "I often wonder what happened to my foster siblings. I was close to one girl, Sheila. We lost touch. I don't know where she ended up."

Violet smiled at Nell. "It's hard, and some people don't want to have reminders of their pasts. I'm grateful for mine, but I understand folks who aren't."

"Me too," Nell said.

Doug finished up Mila's makeup with a flourish. "Ta-da! Want to take a look?" He pulled out a compact with a frown. "I wish I had a bigger mirror—"

"I have one," Luther said. "It didn't sell today. Come on over, sweetheart."

Mila stood and went over to Luther, taking hesitant steps. She stopped in front of him and tilted her head to look up at him.

"Let's see," he said, gently grasping her chin and turning her face from side to side. "That looks great on you. Come here," he said. He pulled a large mirror down from his display panel and held it in front of her. "What do you think?"

Luther wasn't smiling but his eyes...they were full of love for this little girl.

Doug's relationship with his father had been fraught with stress. He knew he had daddy issues, but in his mind, awareness was half the battle. But standing there looking at a guy who likely had some sort of a problematic family situation, being such a good father himself, gave Doug a spark of hope that took him by surprise. Family tableaus hadn't ever elicited much emotion from him in the past other than *wow, that's cool*. But watching Luther be so openly loving with this delicate little girl brought forth a swell of emotion that rocked Doug's foundation.

And made him that much more determined that by the end of the day, he would make sure they didn't wait until the next market to see each other again.

"You like it?" Doug asked as moved to her side.

She looked up at him and grinned, nodding. "It's so pretty."

"Pretty makeup for a pretty girl. I'm glad you like it." Doug turned to smile at Luther, maybe hoping for a compliment from the stoic man.

Instead, he got that full smile he'd been hoping for—and it did wonders to cure the sour mood he'd started to dip into a few minutes before.

FIVE

L uther

Luther couldn't help but bask in the gratitude he felt, watching his foster daughter walk around his booth with a little extra confidence. He'd rested the large mirror against the pole so she could still see herself. She'd move to the tables and straighten the items that hadn't yet sold, which weren't many, and then she'd sneak a peek in the mirror.

Doug had gone back to his booth to put his makeup away, and Luther was frustrated that he needed to stay put. There were still customers coming by, and he really hoped to sell as much as possible so he would have less to lug home, but he wanted to talk to Doug.

Violet had poked him as Doug carefully applied makeup to Mila's face.

"You need to, at the absolute very least, get this man's

number. I don't think he could be any clearer that he's feeling you, LuLu."

He crossed his arms over his chest and sighed. "He's...fun. I don't know. What do I know about fun?"

She snorted. "You used to be fun. You could be fun again."

"What about Mila?" he asked quietly.

Violet gave him a look as if Luther hadn't a clue whatsoever.

"You know as well as I do what your foster parent training said. 'It's important to maintain friendships and a robust support network when taking a child into your home. Set a good example for them by modeling healthy relationships with peers and family.' You know how to model healthy relationships, Luther."

"But when? I can't ask you to watch her any more than you already do."

Violet rolled her eyes. "You definitely can, but also, she's going to summer camp this week, right? Meet him after you drop her off. See what happens when you can actually have a conversation without interruptions. He seems like a good guy."

Luther grunted in agreement. "I'll think about it."

And then he was slammed for the rest of the afternoon, as if a huge wave of afternoon shoppers had just been admitted to the market. Violet took Mila to check out the other vendors when he became too busy to talk to them.

By the time he'd finished with the last of the customers, his neighbors already had their booth packed up and were leading the dogs out of the area.

Luther didn't want to embarrass himself by running after him—not that he could move that fast—but he walked to the end of his booth, hoping to catch Doug's eye.

They'd already made it halfway down the aisle.

He let out a big sigh as he felt a buzz from his phone. It was a new email from—

"Doug at CrossCyber dot com?"

Luther opened the email, and his lips quirked as he read.

Dear Luther,

Thank you for placing your email address on your receipts from the payment app. Pardon my intrusion, but I'd planned on communicating with you prior to my departure, however, transportation demanded that I leave without achieving my objective.

I would like to schedule an appointment with you as your schedule permits to discuss our shared interests. I can be reached by replying to this email, or you can find additional contact information in the signature.

I hope you had a successful venture today, and I look forward to hearing from you.

Warmest Regards,

Douglas D. Cross – B.S. M.A. Cybersecurity

So Doug was a consummate professional in addition to being a phenomenal artist and great with kids and dogs alike. He was beginning to look like the whole package.

Luther, however, wasn't great with pretty words, and typing out an email would have taken him fifteen minutes. He wanted to hear Doug's voice.

He touched the phone number at the bottom of the email and tapped the pop up to put the call through.

"Doug Cross, can I help you?" he answered.

"I think you might be able to. What exactly would you like

to discuss regarding our shared interests?" Luther didn't have much time. Violet and Mila could be back at any minute, but this was fun. There it was again, that concept of fun that Luther thought he'd forgotten how to experience.

"Oh, *hello*, Mr. Sorenson. Thank you for your speedy reply." Doug's voice was dripping with playfulness. "I really had hoped to discuss those interests in person. Do you have any availability—"

"What does your Monday look like?" Luther was already getting impatient. This was fun and all, but he was ready to take things up a notch.

"Hmmm. Monday. I have a client meeting at eight, which should last around an hour. The rest of my day is...flexible."

The word flexible coming through the line had Luther's insides shifting. They were having an innocent enough conversation, but his imagination had kicked into gear and was moving into certain territories sooner than he should allow.

"I drop Mila off at camp at nine."

"Where? I mean, what city?"

"Union City. We're in South Hayward, but she goes to school in Union City. They have a good summer program."

"Excellent. Tell me where you want me. To meet me. Um..." Doug chuckled, which covered Luther's startled gasp.

"Oh, there's a good breakfast place by me. Amy's?"

"Sounds great."

"Nine-thirty?"

"Absolutely," Doug breathed into the phone. "I don't think I've looked forward to a meal this much in a very long time."

Luther knew exactly what he meant.

He was still running through their conversation back in the truck. He caught Violet looking at him funny when he glanced at her in the passenger seat.

"What?"

She tapped her hot-pink nails on her knee. She couldn't wear the acrylics she loved because of work, but she always had her nails painted bright colors.

"I didn't say a word. I definitely didn't say 'I told you.'"

He turned his gaze back on the road and took the exit off the Bay Bridge and onto Interstate 880 South. He allowed himself to contemplate what a date with Doug to discuss "shared interests" would consist of. By the time they pulled into their driveway, he was worrying about what to wear. It was a nice worry to have.

The rest of the weekend was spent watching movies with Mila, making to-do lists to prepare for the next market, meal prepping, and finally, asking Violet for help picking out clothes Sunday evening.

"Oh, honey, we really need to take you shopping. I know this is a casual breakfast, but I want you to feel comfortable. Clothes make the man, don't you know?"

"You're talking to a man who wore a uniform for most of twelve years and who hasn't bought clothes since before that. I've got those clothes Ayana gave me when Hector passed. Maybe there's something nicer in there?"

Violet gave him a sad smile. Hector Barrera had been one of the guys in his unit. He'd been in the same accident with Luther, but he hadn't survived his injuries.

Out of the five soldiers in their vehicle, two had died, one had been able to return to active duty, and two had been permanently disabled. Luther's buddy Carter had been in the passenger seat and he'd lost his right arm in the accident. They'd pushed each other to make it through rehab and had come out the other side functioning humans but no longer working Marines. Carter was doing great. He'd gotten married and was a personal trainer now back in his hometown in Minnesota. He'd been awesome about sending Luther work-outs and checking in on him about his progress.

Most of the guys struggled with how to treat their wounded friends, and Luther understood. For the same reason he hadn't allowed himself to think about the sacrifices he might have to make, they didn't want to have their mortality shoved in their faces.

"Let's go through them together on my next day off. I know she said there were suits in there. Maybe we get stuff dry cleaned so it's ready, you know, for a follow-up appointment." Luther showed her Doug's email, and she cracked up over his formality.

"This seems out of character for the guy who wears a kilt and painted rainbows on Mila's face," she said with a laugh.

She promised to clear out of the house for the day in case their "brunch business meeting" needed to continue at another location. Luther appreciated her cooperation.

He didn't mention it, but there was a part of him that hoped their meeting *would* extend beyond brunch. Mila's camp went until three. She was excited to spend the week making art, going swimming at the high school pool, and watching movies, She'd been thrilled when she found out they were going to be showing *Encanto* at some point. Her full day of fun gave Luther several hours to...meet.

Thankfully ED hadn't been one of the side effects of his injury as the doctors had warned him might happen.

Thank the lord for average-sized mercies.

The next morning, Mila had her hands on her tummy when she came out of her room and was quiet over breakfast.

"What's up, sweetheart?" Luther asked her, tapping the hand on her tummy. Most of the time all she needed was to voice her worries and then the ache went away.

"What if I don't know how to do the projects?"

"You do the best you can and forget the rest. This isn't school, sweetheart. You aren't being graded."

She nodded, looking down at her lap. "What about swimming?"

They'd talked about it, and he'd reassured her that the camp was for kids of all abilities.

"You can just dip your feet if that's all you want to do. I'll look into swim lessons, too, okay?"

She nodded again. "What if I need help?"

He squeezed her shoulder. "You can talk to any of the counselors. They have my number if there's an accident, and I will be there before you're released, understand? Your friend Angela will be there, remember her mommy called me? The two of you can hang out. The day is going to go by super-fast." He was almost more nervous than her, but he had to trust in the camp director's promise that the staff had several kids who came from vulnerable situations and there was extra staff on for the first day to help the kids who were struggling. Miss Vanessa hadn't been worried.

She nodded once more and then took a few more hearty bites of her oatmeal, finished her milk, and ate her sausage patty in two bites.

The drive didn't take long and they were early. He walked her inside the community center, reminded her where the bathrooms were, and helped her stash her lunch in her cubby. It had been such a foreign thing to do—getting a little girl ready for school in the morning—when she first came to live with him, but Luther thrived on routines and soon had it all figured out.

He bent down as much as he could, breathing through the twinge in his back.

"You got this, Mila. I can't wait to hear all about it when I pick you up."

She looked him straight in the eye, furrowed her brow just a little, and gave him a curt nod. "I got this, Daddy."

She threw her arms around his neck, squeezed really hard for about three seconds, and then she let go. Angela and her mom came in at that moment and Mila ran over to her friend. They immediately went over to the toy section and got busy. Luther called out goodbye and got a faint wave in response.

Good. This was good.

"I swear I'm going to nap for the next five days," Angela's mother Felicia said with a laugh as they walked out to the parking lot together. "How about you?"

He grinned at her. "I'm meeting a friend for brunch."

She fist bumped him and they waved to each other as they climbed into their respective cars and sped off for a kid-free day of adult activities.

Luther parked in front of Amy's Diner and sat for a moment, taking a deep breath for courage. He didn't see Doug yet, but he figured he could get them a table. It was a small place, only four or five tables and a counter, but Amy was a legend in the community and her food was to die for. She greeted Luther with a smile and told him to take any open spot.

He headed to the back corner and started to sit down at a table for two when he heard his name. He turned and frowned at the guy who spoke to him. He was brunet, had a pleasant smile, and eyes so strikingly—

"*Doug?*"

Doug held his hands out and gave a small shrug before gesturing for Luther to sit down.

"I know, I know, it's unsettling, isn't it? I usually don't wear makeup for my business meetings. As far as society has come in regards to letting folks be who they are, clients looking to me to handle their companies' security needs don't quite get it."

"You...you look so different. I'm sorry, I didn't recognize you."

Luther liked how Doug looked softer without the sharp angles he created with his makeup, which enhanced his cheekbones and jawline. Today, Luther was in love with the pale pink of his lips, his natural smile. Made-up Doug was drop-dead gorgeous. Softer Doug made Luther relax, feel safe. He imagined what Doug would look like fresh from sleep—or other bed-adjacent activities—and he shivered.

"It's all good," Doug said. "How did camp drop-off go?"

"Good," Luther said, taking a look at the menu, although he always got the same thing. "Typical first-day nerves, but her friend is doing the camp with her. That makes it better, I think."

"For sure. I was an only child, so I had to do all the first days by myself. It made me work hard at finding friends, entertaining people. Probably I was the class clown from about fifth grade on?"

"I can see that," Luther said, his lip quirking up on the side. "I was all about not being noticed in school. Made it easier."

A young man came over with an order pad and gave a very well-rehearsed introduction and asked if they were ready to order. Luther was starving. He'd been too nervous to eat that morning, though he'd tried not to show Mila.

"Waffles with fruit," he said quietly.

"Veggie omelet, please," Doug said. "Hold the onions?"

The kid nodded and scurried away from the table.

"So how long has Mila been with you?"

The kid brought them waters and Luther had just taken a drink when Doug asked his question. He dribbled a little bit of water onto the heather-gray t-shirt he was wearing. It was the only t-shirt he could find that didn't have any holes or logos on it. He'd paired it with navy blue khakis and his only pair of canvas sneakers that weren't stained or ripped. And now he had water stains down the front. *Here's hoping I don't drop my food all over as well.*

"Just about nine months now."

Doug smiled. "She seems happy."

Luther sighed. "She's come a long way. There's been a steep learning curve for both of us."

"I think it's awesome," Doug said. "She's a lucky girl."

"I'm the lucky one."

The server showed up and dropped off their plates, not sticking around to see if they needed anything else. The place wasn't completely full, but he was also helping Amy behind the counter.

"This looks amazing," Doug said. "It's been awhile since I haven't cooked for myself. I'm staying at Dinah's family farm and trying to earn my keep since they won't let me pay rent. I keep telling them I can afford it, but they won't listen. They prefer having a cook and someone to help with barnyard chores, I guess."

"A farm, huh? Nearby?"

"Yeah. It's off Norris Canyon Road? You know, between Castro Valley and San Ramon?"

Luther nodded as he took a bite of strawberry. "I know the area."

"Yeah, Dinah's uncle left the farm to her and her sisters, and they raise goats and chickens and they've got the rescue dogs out there. It's wild. Always some sort of entertainment."

"I can imagine," Luther said. "So Cross Cyber? That's your company?"

"Cybersecurity, yeah." He shrugged. "It pays the bills. Actually right now it's funding my nest egg, since I don't really have many bills."

"Important work," Luther said, and then he chuckled. "At least I'm guessing it is? I don't know much more than basics on the computer. Sometimes I could kick myself that I went the more hands-on direction in the service. It would have been nice to have some transferable skills."

Doug wiped his mouth and set his napkin down. "This is where I ask what's okay to ask about. As a curious person by nature, I have a zillion questions, but I also don't want this date to feel like an interrogation."

Luther fought to hide his grin at Doug's use of the word "date" to describe this encounter. Instead, he let his fork hang in the air.

"Date? I thought we were having a business meeting."

SIX

D^{oug}

Doug's stomach dropped in the split second it took for Luther to smile after that comment. It must have shown on his face, because Luther nudged Doug's foot under the table.

"I'm teasing, sorry. I haven't been on a date in years, so I'm a little rusty."

"Years?" Embarrassment forgotten, Doug leaned closer. "Wait, was it because of your service?"

Luther shrugged. "Only because I was deployed for most of the last four years of my career, and then I was injured." He cleared his throat and his smile turned sad.

"I'm sorry." Doug crossed his leg and found Luther's calf with his foot. He ran his foot along the curve. "I would imagine it would have been tough to be out in the Marines?"

Luther shrugged, still with that hint of a smile. "It's all right. I was discreet. The guys in my unit knew. I didn't really care if people found out. I think it helped that people knew I had their backs. Over there, you needed that."

"I bet," Doug murmured. "I was never deployed abroad but I saw stuff...I handled information, knew what was happening on the ground. I can't... Still can't talk about it, but yeah, it stayed with me."

Luther's smile slipped and his gaze became laser focused, honed in on this shared experience of theirs. Different, but the same. A period of their lives where they saw and heard unspeakable things.

"You can ask me anything," he said in a low voice. They were both leaning forward, the intensity pulling them together despite the table between them. Doug still had his foot linked behind Luther's calf, Luther's other foot was planted against Doug's. Their knees touched. Above the table, passersby would think they were just having a deep conversation, but their entangled limbs below the surface kept them grounded in the moment.

"What was your MOS?"

"K-9," Luther said, clearing his throat again. He took a sip of water and his gaze flicked around the restaurant, likely to see if anyone was invested in their conversation. "MP first, then Military Dog Handler course at Lackland Air Force Base."

"That's...wow, I've heard that's an amazing experience."

Luther looked down at his food. "Most important thing I've ever done, before Mila anyway."

"Do you think that's something you'd want to do as a civilian?"

Luther's face fell and he ate a few bites before he answered. "I don't know if I could work with dogs again."

Doug didn't give a damn. He reached under the small table and put a hand on Luther's knee. "Hey, sorry. We don't have to talk about anything—"

"It's okay. I'd rather get it over with." He cleared his throat again. Man, he was struggling, but Doug admired his willingness to be so open. He wondered what he'd done to deserve such an honor. "I lost my dog in the accident that ended my career."

Doug's breath caught. What was an amazing experience for many often turned into a crushing loss if they lost their K-9 companions.

"Two huge losses," he said quietly. He fanned himself to keep the tears from spilling.

Luther gazed at him with his head tilted, a smile ghosting his lips.

"Thank you. And now we hit on why I was such an asshole the day we met."

"What? No, you weren't. Really."

Luther ate a bite of his fruit and cut up a bit of his waffle. Doug worried his food would be getting cold and felt bad keeping him talking, though he didn't want him to stop, now that he'd started.

"No, no. I insist," Luther said, smiling around his food. "Besides having a particularly difficult pain management day, I wasn't quite prepared for what felt like your blasé attitude about leaving the service. I've since changed my opinion."

Doug sat back and put his hands on the table. "Blasé? Because I did my six and quit?"

"Which is completely understandable. It wasn't what you wanted for your life. We kind of committed ourselves to serving our country so people could have the freedom to make choices like that."

"But Luther, I—"

"It's none of my business why you left, Doug. Really. It's not my place to feel any kind of way about it. It was just hard to hear that when I'd been all kinds of salty that I didn't get my choice."

Doug had worried they were going to be back at an impasse again, but Luther had spilled his whole guts out on the table. Doug had never met a Marine who was this emotionally mature and open about their beliefs. Not that they weren't out there, but frankly, most of the men he'd met along his journey weren't very mature, period. Himself, at times, included.

"You wanted a career."

"Yeah," Luther said, just above a whisper. "I've had the last two years and some change to get used to the fact that it isn't happening. Now I'm just trying to get strong enough to be able to do something else."

"The art is a necessity then, huh?"

Luther nodded. "Well, we're making it, but I want more for Mila. The market will hopefully help with extras."

Doug's face heated, and he leaned forward, folding his elbows on the table. "I know this is going to sound all kinds of wrong. Firstly, I think that's beautiful, and she's lucky to have you. Second...that's *really* hot."

Luther burst out laughing, and his cheeks turned the most lovely shade of red. It was splotchy, like the insides of a pomegranate, and Doug wondered if Luther's skin would taste as tart and sweet.

"That's...thank you." He rubbed at his face, but that only succeeded in making his skin redder, and his blush was... perfect. "To be honest, I was similarly torn watching you do her makeup." He pressed his lips together as if he weren't sure he should admit what he was about to admit. "It was sweet, and you were so good with her. It was also sexy as hell."

Doug was fanning himself again, this time for a very different reason.

They stared at each other for several long moments. Their half-eaten breakfasts had lost their attention.

"Do you want...?"

"Yeah," Luther admitted. "I was kind of hoping. Is that bad?"

Doug pulled out his wallet, stood from the table, and dropped more than enough cash next to his plate to cover their breakfasts. "I'd say my place, but only if you're into barnyard animals, and that would be weird."

Luther snorted. "I'm just around the corner."

"Good. That way you're close in case, you know. I...uh, do we need supplies?"

Luther's brows furrowed. "I hadn't thought of that."

"I'll go," Doug offered. "Here, just put your address into your contact here, and I'll meet you. Any requests?"

"Um, whatever you like to drink? I don't have much at the house. No alcohol, though—"

"Wouldn't dream of it," Doug said. He thoroughly understood the trust involved for Luther to bring someone home, even if Mila wasn't at the house. Man, he was honored.

They split up in the parking lot, exchanging heated glances, and Doug ran over to the Rite Aid across from the restaurant. He wandered a few aisles impatiently before he found the necessary supplies. It had been a while since he'd needed to make such a purchase. He had a fleeting thought that *wow*, he hadn't even kissed Luther yet. Would they be physically compatible? Doug was vers, it depended on the partner, and usually he could tell what was expected, but Luther didn't give off any particular energy. Hell, maybe he just needed a hug and all this would be for nothing. He hadn't asked Luther what his specific disability was, and he certainly didn't want to do anything to make him uncomfortable.

Jesus, he was having a crisis of conscience in the fucking condom aisle.

He brought his purchases up to the counter and realized his worst nightmare.

The old guy at the register, bless his heart, moved at a

glacial pace as he scanned the bottles of root beer, 7Up, and Diet Coke Doug had put on the conveyor belt. Then he got to the two bottles of lube—Doug didn't know if Luther would prefer water or silicone-based—and he peered at Doug over his glasses before scanning and placing them in the bagging area.

Then, of course, the condoms wouldn't ring up.

"Do you happen to recall the price on these?" the man asked.

"No, sorry."

"Mm-hm."

The old man pushed his glasses up to his forehead and brought the condoms so close to his face, Doug thought he might kiss the box. He started calling out the numbers on the bar code one at a time and typing them in.

Meanwhile, there was a line of five people behind Doug who were growing more impatient with each passing minute. Luther probably wouldn't have had any issues. Luther had it so together, he was such an *adult*. Not that Doug wasn't. At thirty, he ran a successful business and had amassed a decent-sized investment portfolio. But he had no home; he'd lived out of his car and short-term rentals for the past three years since he'd set out on his own. Seeing the life Luther had built had Doug feeling...inadequate, and this confounding condom fiasco wasn't helping.

The old man tried three times before he called Irv—no lie, the other employee's name was Irv—and sent the younger man to Aisle Nine to find the price.

"Apologize for the delay," the old man finally said. Then he smiled.

Doug was incredibly tempted to make some blatantly homosexual crack, but that would not help the cause.

Irv was triumphant in finding the price and he and the old man—his name was Dave—took several more tries before they got it entered. Doug tapped his credit card, grabbed the bag and darted out the door as quickly as possible without looking like he'd just shoplifted and was making a getaway.

Nothing like a little condom ridicule to put him back in the teenage terror mindset.

He jogged to his Honda Pilot and tossed the bag into the passenger seat, taking a moment to run his fingers through his hair and let out a growl of frustration. The trip took way too long.

He pulled up Luther's address and started the car, grateful that he lived only a couple of blocks away. He had to pass the house a couple of times before he found a place to park. He dashed out of the car, then had to run back and grab the bag from the store. He was speed-walking up the path when Luther opened the front door.

"Get lost?"

He leaned against the doorframe, his arms crossed over his chest, making his biceps pop, and he had a crooked smile going that stopped Doug in his tracks. That smile made everything he'd just been through worth it.

"I was thwarted by an old man and a faulty barcode. I could have used a Marine, actually."

Luther pushed off the doorjamb and gestured for Doug to enter.

"Come on in and use a Marine, then."

Doug was so focused on Luther's mouth that he tripped going up the last step and had to catch himself on the door frame so he wouldn't crash into Luther.

"Steady there, Airman Doug," Luther chuckled.

Doug made it inside and turned as Luther shut the door, leaning his back against it.

"My sister is out for the day. I have to leave at two-fifteen to pick up Mila."

It was currently ten-forty a.m.

Doug exhaled and grinned. "And I'm yours for the duration."

Luther pushed away from the door and Doug noticed he was barefoot. That made him the same height as Doug, who was wearing slip-on loafers. He kicked them off in case this was a no-shoe household. Luther stood before him, so close their chests brushed, causing Doug to suck in a breath. He thought, *this is it.* He ran his tongue over his lips as a shiver ran through him—

And Luther slid the bag out of his hand.

He stepped into the kitchen area, set the bag on the counter and peeked inside.

"Thanks, man. I haven't had root beer in a while." He pulled the bottle out, twisted the cap off and took a long sip, drawing Doug's gaze to the movement in his throat. All that tawny skin Doug couldn't wait to get his hands on, but he remained motionless. He wanted Luther to make the call.

"That one was for me," Doug teased.

Luther tipped his head back and took another drink, licking his lips before he set the bottle on the counter next to him, keeping his hand on it.

"Come and get it."

Doug was so turned on, he was vibrating. Luther was an entirely different enigma in his own space, and Doug thought he just might be in over his head. He took a step closer.

"Before I do, and I will, I want to make it clear that I'm down for anything, even if that means just talking, or maybe getting a tour of your studio."

Luther gazed at him thoughtfully, but Doug couldn't read his expression. He took a chance, approached the counter, and reached for the bottle. Luther let him take it, and Doug leaned his front against the counter and took his own long drink.

Luther moved behind him, crowding him. He leaned close and ran his nose along the side of Doug's throat, his breath hot against his skin, the movement stirring the hair on the back of his neck. He pressed his chest against Doug's back and put his hands on either side of his on the counter, letting Doug feel that even though they were close to the same size, Luther was bigger. Stronger, despite any physical limitations he might have. And that energy Doug hadn't been able to read earlier? Luther was definitely serving take-charge, as if the alpha male side of him the Corps shaped and molded wasn't completely gone. What a delightful surprise.

Luther kept his hips at a distance as he nibbled and kissed Doug's neck moving from one side to the other, until Doug shuddered and broke out in goose bumps.

"Ticklish?" Luther asked, his soft, calm voice close to his ear.

"I guess so," he admitted, letting his head fall forward. He wanted to turn, wanted to kiss Luther, but he wasn't giving him room to maneuver. He sucked in a breath as Luther planted a hand on the waistband of his jeans. "Or I'm just really turned on. Luther," Doug moaned. He tried to push his hips back into him, but Luther held him in place. He was really fucking strong.

"Give me a minute," Luther said, his voice a little huskier. "It's been a really long time since I've touched someone."

Doug wondered if it had been since his accident, but he certainly didn't want to bring it up.

Luther ran the fingers of his other hand through the back of Doug's hair, gently pulling his head back. "You're beautiful, you know that?"

Doug chuckled. He hadn't expected him to say that.

"Thank you. You're kind of pretty yourself."

"I thought you were gorgeous with your makeup on," Luther breathed. "But today you're...*more*."

Luther's fingers tightened in his hair, but not painfully. Doug gasped and his back arched.

"Listen," Luther started, his voice lower, shaky. "I don't know how this is going to work, okay? I mean, I know my dick works, but my...I fractured my pelvis in the accident. Was in a pelvic external fixator for eight weeks. The doctors told me I'd be lucky if I ever walked again, among other things I don't want to even think about. Bottom line is, I've got arthritis, nerve damage, and I can't bear a lot of weight. My legs get weak."

Doug hated that Luther felt like he had to tell him these things, but he didn't want to interrupt him and say it didn't matter, because it did. The more Doug knew, the better he could take care of him.

"The good news for you," Luther continued, this time pressing his pelvis into Doug's ass, eliciting a moan from him, "is that I love to give more than receive, so whatever happens, I'm going to work hard." He said that last with a little extra emphasis. "I'm gonna make you feel good, Doug."

"Jesus Christ, you're turning me inside out and we still have our clothes on."

Luther gave a very satisfied chuckle, and Doug's knees buckled. Luther shifted his weight and slid his hand down the front of Doug's hip bone, digging his fingers in enough to make him want to beg, but for what he didn't know.

"Is that what you want?" Luther asked. "Clothes off?"

Doug swallowed hard, trying not to pant. "I want to kiss you."

Luther spoke against Doug's ear. "Kissing, huh? I suppose that's all right. Especially since you'll taste sweet after drinking my root beer."

"*My* root beer," Doug retorted, and this time Luther let him turn around.

Up this close, Doug could barely breathe. Luther's gaze was so intense, somewhere between laser focused on completing his mission, curiosity and lust. Doug wanted to hand over all the decisions to this man. He had a feeling it would be that much sweeter.

Instead of kissing him, though, Luther took him by the hand and stepped back.

"Grab the root beer."

Doug snatched the bottle off the counter and reached for the plastic bag with a spare finger as Luther tugged him forward and down the hallway, toward what Doug hoped would be a nice, soft, horizontal surface for them to continue this parlay.

SEVEN

L uther

Luther was surprisingly *not* nervous. Doug had let him set the pace and that meant he could take his time. That freedom let him worry less about how his body was going to respond, now that he was about to have a sexual experience with another person for the first time in three years. *Finally.*

He was *so* fucking hard, but he wasn't feeling that desperation that used to come with sex. He hadn't had a steady in about ten years, not since his on-again, off-again boyfriend Gary, and even then, his schedule rarely allowed for slow, languorous afternoons in bed. He'd been in a hurry for most of his life, honestly, never able to savor the good things. One of the blessings of his accident meant that he'd had to learn patience. It hadn't been a pretty lesson, but he was appreciating it more than ever as he led Doug down the hallway.

"Love the colors in here," Doug said, glancing around the

hallway and into the open doors of the bathroom and Mila's room at the splashy paintings Luther had done at Violet's request. She'd wanted paintings with big, bold, colors, and he'd given her whatever she wanted. Each room in the house had a different color scheme, and he'd done paintings to reflect her choices, so every room had turned out bright. Luther loved it, especially when the three of them planned out what colors to use for Mila's room. Yellows and oranges, the colors of the sun. That had been a fun weekend.

"Thanks. Violet's in charge of the interior design. Every-where except my room."

He opened the door and was grateful he'd put clean sheets on the bed that morning. His room contained a simple dark wooden queen-size bed frame and a large chest of drawers shoved into one side of the closet. He had a weight bench and his exercise mat against the wall. The bedspread was navy, sheets and pillows all navy, and the walls were painted a soft cream.

He kept his space spotless; it helped with the clutter in his mind to have a clear space to think and do his exercises. He had to pass his mat to get out the door, so he had no excuse not to do them. He'd always loved exercise. That was, until it became a necessity for existence.

"Oh," Doug breathed. "Luther, that's so awesome."

His attention was on the wall he'd decorated with Mila's art. Everything she'd done at school, every drawing, every painting she'd done in the studio, it was all hanging on cork-board panels on the wall interspersed with pictures of her.

"I want to celebrate all of her wins."

The only other decor in the room was on the wall above his exercise area. It had taken him a bit, but he'd finally decided to hang up pictures of the guys in his unit, hang up his folded flag in the frame, pictures of Bunker and his vest, which his buddies had mounted in a shadow box, along with their medals. It was a reminder of what he'd accomplished, and now he could look on it as motivation to get better instead of continuous grieving.

"Your dog was so handsome."

Luther sighed. "Thanks. He was the best boy."

Luther took the bottle of root beer and set it on the bedside table, and then he turned to Doug. He ran his knuckles down Doug's soft midsection. He loved that he was unapologetic about his body, from the clothes and makeup he wore to the fact that he was healthy but not obsessed with fitness. While Luther missed his own six-pack, he appreciated body types of all kinds, especially now.

He slid his two fingers under Doug's waistband, ready to strip him down. "When I ask you what you want, I want the truth, not what you think *I* want, what you think is the right answer. I want pure, unadulterated Dougish desires right now." He slid his fingers gently over the swell below Doug's belly button. "Tell me what you want."

Doug's eyes fluttered closed and he swayed closer to Luther.

"First I want to kiss you. Then I want to get you off," he whispered as Luther flicked open his button. "I want you all over my face," he moaned, as Luther pulled down his zipper. "I want to taste you all over. That's for starters." He ran his fingers up Luther's arms and rested them on his shoulders.

Luther licked his lips and went in for a kiss he hoped would be good enough for Doug to want a second, a third. Kissing had always been awkward for Luther. He'd liked it fine, thought he did a satisfactory job, but with Doug, he wanted to make it more than good, so memorable that whatever happened next, he'd be glad he came home with Luther.

Doug sighed happily and gripped Luther's shoulders tighter. Here was the Doug he'd seen dancing, singing, and smiling as if he were darn happy to be alive the first time they'd met. He'd been a little subdued all morning, maybe even a little nervous, but under Luther's touch, he came alive. He was *excited,* and that supercharged Luther's arousal.

Luther kept the kiss light, but he was already intoxicated with Doug's mouth. He'd known before he invited him back to his house that this was just the beginning. He'd need more than one tryst with this devilishly pretty man. Luther pulled back slowly, teasing with his tongue as he ended the kiss.

Doug opened his eyes, his lids heavy, and tilted his head. "What do you want, Luther?" he whispered.

Luther chuckled softly and ran his free hand over his mouth, which was watering thinking about Doug's request. Then he rested his hands on Doug's hips, anxious to unwrap his gift.

"I want you naked and thrashing on my bed in total abandon. I want messy hair. I want sweat. I want to taste your cum." He slid his hands into Doug's pants, hissing when he found bare skin. "And if I'm not too wrecked at that point, I'll want to start all over again."

Doug's pants hit the ground, and Luther grinned at the sight of his long, tattooed, muscular legs. Doug reached for the hem and pulled off his shirt, apparently impatient with Luther's pace. Then he stepped out of the pants gracefully and slide his socks off. He was wearing designer underwear in a jockstrap cut, and Luther wanted to thank whoever thought that was a good idea when he got a look at Doug's bare, round ass with the straps running underneath.

Doug scooted the pile of clothes out of the way and cocked a hip out. "What's next?"

Luther reached around him and pulled the blankets back, folding them over at the foot of the bed. "Lay back."

Doug sat and scooted back, laying his head on the pillow on the far side, his arm folded behind his head. Luther wanted to look his fill at Doug's mostly hairless body. *He must shave.*

That's hot.

Luther let out a breath and shook his head. "I want to keep looking, but I also want to start touching."

Doug laughed and slid his free hand down his stomach, hooking his thumb on the elastic of his underwear. He knew just how good he looked and how he was affecting Luther. Not that it was hard to tell. Luther's erection was pressed almost painfully against his pants, the tip caught under his waistband.

He grasped the back collar of his t-shirt and pulled it off over his head. And then he paused again. There was a part of him that wanted to crawl into bed with Doug, skin-to-skin, and let himself be held. Let someone else bear his weight for a little while.

But he also wanted to worship Doug's body, right down to those perfect fingers and toes. He wanted to trace all of his tattoos with his tongue, wanted to—*fuck*—wanted to suck those nipple piercings into his mouth until Doug did exactly as Luther wanted...thrashed on the bed until he came.

He blew out a breath. "This is the part I'd like to get over with quickly." He didn't want to put on a show. He just wanted to get out of his clothes and move on to the good part. He pulled his pants down and slowly lowered himself to a sitting position on the bed. "I'll try not to make old-man noises, but sometimes it can't be helped."

Thankfully he didn't struggle getting the pants off his legs, but then he had a twinge when he scooted and attempted to lay back without a grunt. He failed. Once he was flat next to Doug, he let out a breath.

"And *that* is how a thirty-five-year-old man in an eighty-year-old's body gets down."

Doug laughed and turned onto his side to face Luther. "I'm into it," he said, blowing his hair up out of his eyes. "I think old men are hot, especially when they make old-man noises. No, I'm serious," he said, placing a hand on Luther's chest when he groaned. "I'd take an old man over a young guy any day. Especially one who's got such delectable skin. May I sample?"

Luther turned his head to face him. "In a minute. I'm waiting for my second wind and then hold on to your dentures. We're gonna party like it's the late nineteen hundreds."

Doug burst out laughing and rolled onto his back, which gave Luther the perfect opportunity to roll on top of him.

And then it was on.

Luther had an out-of-body experience, at least as far as the pain was concerned. It was forgotten beyond the throb of longing in his groin. Doug moaned hungrily as Luther settled between his open thighs. They devoured each other's mouths as they explored with their hands. Luther quickly divested Doug of his delightful undergarment and purred over the sight of his veiny, gracefully curved shaft and perfectly plump tip. He quickly discovered it tasted as good as it looked, and he proceeded to talk with his mouth full as he extoled its attractive attributes.

Doug, indeed, thrashed about on the bed, his heels digging for purchase in the sheets. Luther placed a hand on his hip to hold him still and laughed when Doug pleaded with him.

"You got thrashing, messy hair, and sweat. If you want my cum, I need you to—*Jesus, Luther. Fuck.*"

Luther added a finger to the mix, which sent Doug into a frenzy. When he cried out for more, Luther complied, and within moments, Doug was, as requested, covered in cum.

Luther rolled onto his back and gloated in his victory. "Still got it," he said with a fist pump while Doug tried to catch his breath.

"That's not fair," Doug said, stretching his arms out toward him. "I didn't even get to touch you yet."

Luther looked up at him and laughed when he saw his adorable pout. "Hang on, it takes a minute to maneuver." He rolled carefully onto his side and attempted to scoot back up the bed. A twinge in his lower back had him stopping to breathe through the spasm. When he got close to Doug, he reached over, grabbed a tissue, and used it to clean up Doug's belly before he collapsed across his chest.

"That's what I'm talking about," Doug said, still panting. "This is the best part."

"Better than that performance? Really?"

Doug brushed his jaw along Luther's head and kissed him. "Okay, second best. Seriously, I'd very much like to reciprocate."

"In a minute," Luther said, his own heart finally slowing to a normal resting beat. "I like this part too."

The next thing he knew, his phone was buzzing on the floor in his pants pocket. The first of the three alarms he'd set to be sure he didn't miss picking up Mila was going off. He had forty-five minutes until he needed to leave.

"I didn't want to wake you," Doug said, his voice sleepy next to Luther's ear. "You were so...relaxed."

Luther turned to face him and smiled. "I was. I am, thank you. Come here." He slipped his fingers behind Doug's neck and pulled him close, licking his way into a deep kiss. Doug sighed and pressed his body flush to Luther's. "We have time if you're up for round two."

Doug ran a hand down Luther's stomach and over the front of his boxer briefs. "Only if you're the one who gets messy this time."

Luther was still in that post-nap dreamy place, so he let Doug roll him onto his back and pull off his boxer briefs.

"Get it over with," Luther said—and Doug froze.

"Get it...*what*?"

Luther smiled down at him, brushing his hair out of his face. "The cringe, the gasp, the 'oh my God, you poor thing' comments. That's all I've heard from caregivers and my sister once they saw my scars. I know, it's an ugly mess."

Doug stared up at him, his brow furrowed. "Luther."

Luther cupped his jaw. "I don't know what will happen," he said. "But I'm as relaxed as I'm gonna get."

Doug crawled up Luther's body and straddled his hips, making sure not to put any weight on him. "Does your skin hurt where the scars are?"

It wasn't a pitiful question. Doug seemed to be searching for information vital to his impending activity, almost as if he were trying to do his job to the best of his ability.

"Not really, no."

"How about pressure? Have you had massage work?"

"I...yeah, some. At physical therapy. I haven't had any since I finished my sessions last year. My benefits don't cover massage."

"See, that's where you chose well. I happen to have gone to massage school, and body work is one of my favorite things to do for a partner." Doug grinned at him. "How about ass play?"

Luther smiled. "Love it," he moaned. This was fun. Of course, Doug *would* make it fun. "I went easy on you, but yeah. I love it, giving and receiving."

"Good to know. Now," he said, crawling back down Luther's body. "I take direction well. I insist you tell me if anything isn't feeling okay."

And with that, Doug once again gifted Luther with an out-of-body experience, only this time, Luther went on an emotional ride. He could tell himself all he wanted that he didn't care what he looked like, that it didn't bother him if his partner gaped at the round scars from the contraption that had held his bones in place as they healed, the big round keloids on his front and back, and the staple scars that zigzagged along his hips and thigh. And sure, he'd gotten himself off plenty of times in the interest of ensuring everything still worked. But this? The soft, enveloping warmth of Doug's mouth was something else, his touch steady and firm.

Doug was either being mindful of their time limit, or he was simply zealous about his oral occupation, because there was no teasing, no timid exploration. It was as if he'd taken Luther's cock and told it, "You will bend to my will, and you will enjoy it. You will come when I say."

Luther concentrated on letting his body feel the pleasant, erotic, intense sensations, and when Doug whispered "let go," he did just that. The muscles in his lower back threatened to contract painfully, but he was able to ride it out and let himself experience the joy of sharing intimacy with a caring partner.

The tears, he was not expecting.

Doug lay beside him and turned his face for a deep kiss. Luther enjoyed tasting himself on Doug's tongue.

"Hey," Doug said softly, thumbing a tear away. "What's going on?"

"This?" Luther said, wiping at his face and looking at his hand. "I'm not really sure," he said with a laugh. "Call it a full-body climax, I guess. Apparently I needed to get everything out."

"As long as I didn't hurt you or—"

"God, no. You were exactly what I needed. Thank you," he whispered, going in for another kiss. "Thank you for that awesome re-entry."

"You're very welcome. I'd love to do it again."

He wished they had more time. He wasn't done with Doug.

"How about tomorrow?"

. . .

And that's how Luther and Doug had their own week of summer camp. Doug came over each morning after Luther dropped Mila off at camp, which she loved. She spent every afternoon telling Luther in detail everything they'd done, and she'd made him more artwork for his collection. He spent each evening with her, relaxing on the couch while they watched her favorite Tim Burton movies, and she inevitably fell asleep early every night. The camp had been a great idea. He planned to see if there was another week in August when he could send her. By then, he'd have enough saved up to pay the fee.

Doug and Luther spent late mornings in his bed, they'd have lunch, and then they'd go out to Luther's studio and talk shop. On Thursday, Doug even went with him out to his buddy's property in the North Bay so he could collect more wood for his paintings. The process went by much smoother with Doug there to help, and Luther wasn't paying for it later in the day.

Doug brought his massage oil on Friday morning and proceeded to give Luther the best massage of his life. He could get used to this type of TLC. He *wanted* to get used to this time with Doug.

When it was time for Luther to pick up Mila, he stopped Doug at the entryway.

"I don't think I need to tell you that this has been the best week I've had in maybe forever. I know this was a special occasion because Mila was at camp, but I want to see you. *Keep* seeing you. It'll be different, yeah, but—"

"Oh honey, did you honestly think you'd be getting rid of me after this week? I'm hooked on you. I want to keep seeing you, too." His smile slipped a little. "I have to fly out Monday to do an onsite with one of my clients, but I should only be gone a couple of days. I'd like to have you and Mila out to the farm. I think she'd love it."

Luther's hopeful heart gave a thud. He hadn't counted on finding someone who would so easily accept his daughter and what life with a single dad was like, but with Doug, he had hope.

"I think we'd *both* love it. I do have a thing for barnyard animals."

Doug wrinkled his nose. "You're bad." He threw his arms around Luther's neck and gave him a big wet, sloppy kiss, which Luther loved. Everything about Doug had him completely gone in a way he'd never expected to be.

"And you love it," he said, then his cheeks heated. Had he said too much? Gotten too heavy too soon?

But Doug gave him a wink and kissed him once more before swinging his messenger bag over his shoulder.

"You know I do. I'll call you when I'm back. Text me how Mila's last day at camp went." Doug had wanted a full report each day, and Luther had been surprised how much that meant to him.

"Have a safe trip," Luther called out, watching Doug saunter down the steps. He'd worn his kilt that day. He'd had a lot of fun with Doug in a kilt. He might have mentioned to him that he wouldn't be mad about it if Doug spent *every* day in a kilt.

Luther sighed and closed the door. He only had time to grab his keys and head out to his truck, to think about what a great week they'd had, and how much he hoped it was the first of many.

Part Three
Fall Equinox

EIGHT

D^{oug}

Thoughts of his "summer camp" with Luther kept Doug going over the next three months as his business took him away from his new temporary home for most of that duration. They'd managed to sneak in a couple of dates when Violet had time to stay with Mila, but those had been rushed affairs, merely long enough to catch up, hold hands for a bit, and get into heated make-out sessions before it was time for Luther to get home. They texted a lot, and the time had been good for them to get to know each other a little better, but absence had made Doug's heart grow...anxious.

He'd gone into business for himself in order to have autonomy over where he spent his time, but he also knew that his future ability to support himself depended on laying the groundwork now. Besides, he couldn't just abandon his clients.

When one of the largest tech companies he worked with had a breach in their security during his routine visit to their Denver, Colorado, campus, it was immediately assumed it was a failure on his part. Doug worked night and day to put up new protections and hunt down the culprit. The owner, a woman not much older than him named Omaria Dawson, was patient and trusted him even when her board didn't. It was a good thing she had—because it turned out the breach came from within, from one of her most trusted employees.

Doug promised that he would stay until he'd completely redesigned their security system, investigated the backgrounds of everyone who had access, and spent whatever time it took to train her in-house security team on the new systems and how to keep a closer eye out for unauthorized activity.

Doug had been with Omaria since the beginning of her company's expansion, and she was grateful for his support. Her board approved a hefty sum to compensate Doug for his work once she shared with them the situation, and they approved his continued involvement in the security of their company.

Because of the nature of the breach, Doug contacted his other clients, told them what had happened, and let them know that he had an updated system fix that would protect them from the same thing happening to their assets. They all took him up on his offer to do the on-site work, and he agreed he would only charge his hourly rate. It was an involved yet necessary project that would ensure his business continued to run smoothly, and his reputation wasn't harmed by the security breach.

Unfortunately, he worried his reputation *had* been harmed with a certain single foster dad who waited patiently for him to return. Luther assured Doug that he understood.

"Trust me, I get deployment. Remember? Kind of did it for twelve years."

But the two of them had laid the foundation for something pretty special that first week together, and the longer Doug was away, he wondered if Luther would decide that having a transient boyfriend was too much trouble when he had his own hands full raising an incredible kid.

The weekend of the fall equinox, the Shaw sisters had planned to have a Sapphic Celebration of the Changing of the Seasons, or something to that effect. The name seemed to change depending on who he was talking to, as one-third of the Shaw sisters was not of the lesbian persuasion. They'd invited their extended family and friends, and *their* friends, which meant a boatload of families with kids were coming out to the farm to harvest pumpkins and wildflowers, make bird feeders to tide over the winged friends traveling this time of year, and to eat to their hearts' delight. They'd reserved a special bookmobile to come out, which was owned by a sweet lesbian couple. Doug was excited to check it out as he was an avid reader. The Shaw sisters had also invited Doug's band, the East Bay Goth Punks, to play, which seemed fitting since three-fourths of the band were, in fact, lesbians.

Doug invited Luther, Mila, and Violet to come out, and they graciously accepted, but Doug was still nervous. He hadn't seen Luther in about four weeks, and though he got home with a few days to spare before the event, Luther had been busy with his new job—Campus Monitor at Mila's school—and Doug needed to help his housemates get ready, as well as attend a couple of emergency band practice sessions that had lasted late into the night. He hadn't felt comfortable just dropping by Luther's, but he'd sent flowers. He'd actually sent several little gifts while he'd been gone, and Luther had always said thank you...

But Doug had come to realize how important Luther was in his universe, and he had no idea, after being gone for so long, how to let him know without putting too much pressure on him. It was a delicate dance. Luther had to be careful how he introduced someone new into his life because of Mila. She'd met Doug, and they'd gotten along famously, but did she even know Luther was gay? Doug had so many questions, ones that he hadn't wanted to discuss while they were thousands of miles apart.

Before sunrise on the morning of the Hoedown Honkytonk Hootenanny, as he'd started calling it just to get a rise out of his roommates, he'd started baking. And baking. Usually it calmed his nerves, but there were too many anxious nerves to be cured by cupcakes alone. When he ran out of ingredients to make more muffins, cupcakes, and brownies, he gathered art supplies for the kids and set up the birdfeeder stations. Everything was ready, except him.

What would this night mean for him and Luther?

The guests started arriving at two in the afternoon and Doug spent the next three hours painting faces, chasing escaped goats, and helping kids with the various projects, along with his cousin Matt and his husband Zack. Dinah had a couple of the rescue dogs out of their enclosures and on leashes and was walking them around to meet folks and show the kids what tricks they knew. Cecily was supervising the petting zoo, cousins Marianne and Nell were handling the pumpkins, and Trudy, Dinah's eldest sister, greeted their guests and kept the treats and punch stocked.

By the time the food truck rolled up the driveway at five, there were probably close to seventy or eighty people wandering around the property. So far, it had been a huge success, but Doug began to wonder if Luther and his family were going to make it.

More folks were coming later that night to see the band. Doug's bandmates had set up a stage behind the house, which was the farthest point from the barn. Cecily had been concerned about the noise bothering the animals, and Dinah wasn't sure how the dogs would do. There were three dogs in the new runs, which had been finished two weeks prior. They were doing well, except for one guy they called Oscar, as in The Grouch, because Nell thought he had grumpy eyebrows. He was a massively fluffy shepherd of some sort, no one was really sure, but he was very withdrawn. Not in a fearful way or like he might be aggressive, but he just seemed disinterested in everything and most everyone.

Doug had sat with him for a while that morning, in between baking loads, and he'd gotten the old guy's ears to perk up as he talked to him, but that was about it. Dinah said it was more of a reaction than she'd gotten. She wasn't sure what they were going to be able to do for him, and she'd reached out to some of the shepherd rescues to see if they had advice.

Doug was finishing his last face-painting customer of the day before he was ready to close up shop when he heard the crunch of gravel behind him that signaled tiny running feet.

"Hi Doug. Can I have a turn?"

Doug turned to find a grinning Mila. Beyond her was a waving Violet, and next to her, sporting a cane and moving slowly, was the object of Doug's desire—and dilemma.

"Well, not if you've been kicking your dad in the shins! What's with the cane?" he asked her.

She giggled. "I didn't kick him," she said. "He needs it sometimes when his legs is bad."

Sure enough, Doug noticed that Luther's gait was off. He wanted to run to him, he wanted to—

"Am I done?"

The little boy he'd been painting dragon scales on had been fidgeting for the entire fifteen minutes he'd been sitting there. Doug figured he was as done as he was going to get. He drew one last glittery scale with flourish and waved him away.

"Off you go, you fierce creature."

The kid knocked the chair over in his haste to run over to the pumpkin patch. Mila picked up the chair and sat in it.

"Did you ask if it was okay, sweetheart? Doug might need a break."

Luther stopped next to Doug's chair and smiled down at him.

Oh, he's nervous too.

"I'm so glad you're here," he said, meaning all of them, of course, but he looked directly at Luther as he spoke.

"I'm so sorry we're so late," Violet said, squeezing Doug's shoulder. "I got off late this morning and Luther didn't want to wake me too early. This place is amazing! I've driven past it before and had no idea it was still a working farm."

"Yeah, the sisters have been building it back up. They inherited it from their uncle and by the time they took it over, he was down to a couple of donkeys and chickens that had stopped laying eggs. Cecily's a genius. She brought in new chickens and goats, and now she has a whole thriving business going, making skin care products from the goat milk and selling fresh eggs at the farmer's markets every weekend."

"Can I pet the goats, Daddy?"

Luther smiled down at her. "You want to do that, or do you want your face painted?"

"Oh, my face. Please, Doug?"

"Of course you can. You can do both. What would you like?"

She looked at the board he'd put out with some ideas for the kids, and then she looked at him. "Can I have bat wings like you?"

Doug's cheeks warmed. She was the absolute best. He'd done his makeup hours ago and had no idea whether it was still legible. Apparently it was.

"Bat wings are awesome," Luther said. "You want to tell Doug about the bats we saw at the zoo this week?"

Mila's eyes got big and she began to relay all of the facts she'd learned while Doug made encouraging noises and went to work giving her badass bat wings beside her eyes. She told him all about the flying foxes from Malaysia and how fruit bats are different than the kind of bats that are native to the Bay Area, which eat insects. She was in the process of listing all the types of fruit they ate when Doug finished her second wing off with some extra glitter.

"Well, those bats sound cool and all, but you, my dear, are the coolest bat around." He held up a big mirror to show her and she gasped, pressing her hands over her mouth dramatically.

"I *am* the coolest bat," she breathed. In the next breath, she turned to Luther. "Can I go see the goats now?"

He smoothed down her hair, which had been cut recently, and her bangs were no longer quite so heavy across her brows. It gave her a much more open and expressive face. Doug had an inkling that a lot of that had to do with the time Luther had put in building a relationship with her.

Doug gazed longingly at Luther. He was still so goddamned honored to know the man.

Violet looked between them and took Mila's hand. "How 'bout I take you?"

Mila gave Luther a glance only long enough for him to nod once before she hopped out of the chair and practically dragged Violet over to the barn.

Luther watched them go with a laugh, calling out to Mila, "Be careful." Then he turned and smiled at Doug. "You are a sight for sore eyes."

Doug stood from the chair and wanted to hurl himself at Luther, hold him tight, and never let him go. Luther seemed similarly conflicted.

"Is there somewhere—?"

"Do you need to sit—?"

They both chuckled, and Luther stepped closer to him. "Can we take a walk?"

Doug winced at the cane. "Can we? I don't want you in pain."

Luther wrinkled his nose. "I'm fine. I'm walking a lot more now that I'm working at the school, and sometimes I get tired. It's more a just-in-case kind of thing. Can't be falling down on the job. Come on, show me around."

"You sure you don't want to head straight for the animals?" Doug joked.

Luther took his hand and squeezed. "I'm where I want to be." His smile was hesitant, but his words relieved some of the tension in Doug's shoulders.

"That's good to know," he murmured. He started leading Luther around the back of the barn, where the ground was flatter and they'd have some privacy. "I was worried about... you know..."

Luther glanced around at all the activity and took a few more steps before speaking. "Worried how?"

Doug adjusted his grip on Luther's hand. They hadn't had enough time to do this...just hold hands. They hadn't been able to really go anywhere, have any real dates.

He blew out a breath. "I was gone so long, I thought maybe I'd missed my chance."

"At what?" Luther asked. "I mean, you missed the flower pots I painted for last month's market. Those did really well. And you missed me freaking out over Mila's court date, which went fine. I was nervous for no reason."

"I *bet* you were nervous! I was nervous, too, just hearing about it. You guys are so close."

"Yeah," Luther said, smiling as he looked down at the ground in front of them. "She's pretty awesome. I love being her dad."

Once more Doug was floored by Luther's reality. He'd

sacrificed so much, and by taking on a foster child, he continued to give of himself.

"Her dad's pretty awesome, too."

They'd made it behind the barn, and Doug stopped, drawing Luther close to him.

"The whole time I was gone," he began, "I wished I wasn't. This wasn't typical at all. On a regular basis, the most I'm ever gone is a few days out of the month. I couldn't help but think..." He paused. This was a delicate dance. He didn't want to come on too strong.

"I missed you," Luther breathed, rubbing his thumb over Doug's knuckles. "But it was like you were there. Because you were. You called, you texted. I mean, sure, I wanted more Dougish Desires time, but life kept moving, you know? Mila and I had stuff to do, we did some art classes, then it was back-to-school shopping time, five-oh-four meetings with her school administrators. I got the job...but you were still here," he said, holding their linked hands up and rubbing Doug's knuckles over his chest. "And it was okay."

"God, I missed you, too, Luther. I didn't want to burden you with that, but I missed you so goddamned bad. We only really had that week, you know? And two sort-of dates. It wasn't fair. I didn't want to be adulting halfway across the country, but then I thought about you and how you had no choice but to adult every minute of every day, and I thought... does he need my mess too?"

"Hey," Luther said, shushing him and bringing him in for an embrace that nearly made Doug crumble. It felt too good to hope for. "I do have responsibilities, but it's important that I have a balance in my life. The classes I went through to become a foster parent are clear about that. I wasn't looking for a relationship, but then you showed up, and I wanted it. I *want* it. I want you, Doug." He massaged the back of Doug's neck and pressed their foreheads together.

"Does Mila know you're gay? Does she know about us?"

Luther deflated a little at that and planted his cane next to him. He leaned back against the barn. "I don't know, and not really."

Doug exhaled and his posture matched Luther's. They still held hands, and that made him not panic.

"It hasn't really come up, I guess? I'm out, my friends know, the social worker, lawyer, judge...everyone knows. I just haven't approached the topic with her. It's weird. I don't know a whole lot about her home life before she came to me. She could have come from a super intolerant place. For all I know, she could have heard terrible shit about gay people. I wanted her to feel comfortable with me before it came up. She's only eight, you know?"

"I get it, I do. She could have been like me and grown up in a house where all I heard was how my uncle must have fucked up somewhere along the line to have two gay kids. I love my uncle. I love my cousins. I always wished I could live with them every time they came over for a holiday, even though they were way older than me. Then when they'd leave, I was stuck knowing I was going to disappoint my father no matter what I did, because I just wanted to wear fishnet stockings and lipstick." Luther chuckled, so Doug kept on. "I saw *Rocky Horror* and thought 'that's what I want to be when I grow up.'"

"Tim Curry's hot," Luther said, tugging their hands a little.

"Yeah, and he got the girl *and* the guy wearing that getup. I wanted that. Okay, maybe not the corset, though. I used to wear one with my old band and that shit is uncomfortable. No wonder women used to burn their bras."

Luther was belly laughing now, and Doug breathed a sigh of relief. All hope was not lost.

"Mila loves your makeup. She says it's like in a Tim Burton movie. She loves Johnny Depp."

"That's quite a compliment. I guess she hasn't seen *Rocky Horror* yet?"

"That's a negative, Senior Airman Doug. I might be okay letting her listen to the E Ladies and their talk of being bad girls—"

"The E Ladies?"

"Ella, Etta, and Eartha. Violet plays them all the time and Mila got hooked. There's a lot of jazz in my house, but those three are the trifecta."

"Wow, that's awesome. I love jazz."

"Yeah, well, I like fucking Metallica. Pantera. Megadeth. Loud shit. But I sacrifice, you know. For the ladies."

Doug cupped Luther's jaw and ran a thumb over his lip. "I love it. I like it loud too. In fact, if you stick around for a little while, you'll get to hear some. I'll even be in my fishnets and platforms."

Luther turned to face him and leaned his shoulder against the barn. "That's right. Goth and punk, huh? Interesting intersection."

"Is it really that surprising?" Doug asked. "Maybe one's a little more passive and the other aggressive?"

They smiled at each other for several beats, which did little to ease Doug's worries.

"Can I kiss you?" Luther finally asked breathlessly. "You made me like kissing, dammit. I haven't been able to practice. I might be rusty at it."

Doug grinned and curled Luther's shirt in his fists. "We can't have that."

As the sun began to sink behind the hilltop to the west of the farm, Doug and Luther kissed like men on leave who hadn't seen the object of their desire for months. Things threatened to get heated, but then Doug would hear a child's laugh or the *baaa*ing of a goat, and he'd pull back just a little. He wished he could take Luther up the back steps of the house and into his room.

"What was that?"

In addition to children and goats, another creature made a sound that caught their attention.

"Oh. Maybe it's Oscar. I was going to check on him before the second half of the festivities. Come on. I'll show you what my artistic endeavors have allowed Goth Dog Rescue to purchase."

Doug moved at Luther's pace and when they got around the other side of the barn, he gestured. "Voila. New spacious accommodations for the rescues who need a little more work or some extra time."

Two border collies bounded back and forth, chasing each other on either side of their fences, but the sound Luther had heard came from the occupant of the nearest pen.

"That's Oscar. I was with him this morning for a while. Dinah's trying to get some extra help with him. He just seems so depressed, poor guy, or like he can't be bothered with this world any longer."

Oscar was laying with his legs out front of him, watching the other dogs run back and forth like "are you serious right now?" and every so often, he'd let out a distressed sound, not like he was in pain, but like he was distraught.

Luther approached the chain-link, and Doug stood beside him.

"He hasn't shown any signs of aggression, but no one has really been able to get through to him. He's a beautiful dog, not sure how old he is."

Luther leaned against the fencing and linked his fingers in the chain. He murmured something under his breath—and the dog's head snapped toward him, ears at attention. Luther stood up straighter and spoke again. This time, Oscar got to his feet, turned in a circle, and sat at attention.

"Holy shit," Doug said. "What just happened?"

Luther walked over to the gate to go inside the pen. "May I?"

"Yeah, sure, but let me go in with you, just in case."

Luther snorted. "You *do* know what I did in the Marines?"

"Fuck, that's right, I forgot." Doug chuckled and opened the gate for them and they went inside. Oscar still sat at attention. Luther gave another command—was that German?—and Oscar lay down. Another command, and Oscar crawled forward. At the next command, Oscar came to Luther, walked around behind him and sat on his left side.

"So you're telling me the dog speaks German? Like he hasn't understood us? Explains the grouchy eyebrows."

Luther laughed and reached out a hand to scratch Oscar's ears, and for the first time the dog looked, well, not quite happy, but not so grumpy. His tongue lolled out the side of his mouth as he looked at Luther.

Me, too, Oscar. Me too.

"Some trainers use German commands. Somebody worked with this guy." Luther looked around and noticed the play yard. "Mind if I take him in there?"

At that moment, Dinah came around the corner, and she gasped.

"Did you just get him to *heel*?"

Luther smiled at her, and Doug gestured for her to come over. "He wants to take him into the play yard."

"Sure. Wow, I've been so worried about him." She entered the play yard and opened the gate from the back of Oscar's run. Oscar remained sitting at Luther's side, panting, until Luther gave him a hand signal to go. The dog walked beside him, waiting for the next cue, and when they got inside the play yard, Luther ran him through some of the agility course before he had him heel once more.

"That's amazing," Dinah said, coming forward. She held her hand out for Oscar to sniff, keeping her gaze on Luther. "We tried a few commands with him, but he wasn't treat motivated and he wouldn't respond. I didn't even think to try German. You've obviously worked with dogs before?" The dog let her scratch his ears, but he kept his focus on Luther.

"Military, yeah. Maybe get in touch with someone at Travis Air Force Base, they might have someone there who's looking to adopt."

"I'll do that," Dinah said, but she was smiling as she looked between Luther and Oscar. "He seems to really respond to you."

Luther's cheeks flushed and he gave a crooked smile. "He's great, but I've got a little girl. We're working on getting ourselves squared away right now."

She nodded and sighed. "I get it. I feel like he's had a long journey that led him here. I just hope we can find him a home where he's happy."

Luther gazed wistfully at Oscar and sighed. "Me too."

"I'll just put him back for now. Oh! Hey, Doug? Barb said to let you know you guys are going to start in about forty minutes so you can," she waved her hands around in front of him, "work your magic."

"Thanks," Doug laughed. "I'll be right there."

She called Oscar and he hesitated, giving Luther the saddest eyes before letting out a dramatic groan and following her.

"Wow," Luther said, shaking his head. "Way to make a guy feel guilty."

"Are you kidding? No way. You just did him a solid by proving he's not just a grumpy dude in a garbage can."

Luther laughed and reached for Doug's hand again. "I

know you have to go to do…this," he imitated Dinah, and Doug laughed, pulling him in for a hug.

"I'm so glad you came."

Luther squeezed him tight with one arm, the other still planted on his cane. "Listen," he said. "I'm going to work on talking to Mila. I don't know what will happen, but I want *us* to happen, all right? Can you be patient with an old man?"

Doug held the sides of Luther's face and rubbed noses with him. "Told you, I like old men. And I want that more than anything, as long as you can be patient with me too. I won't have to travel as much from here on out, and now I've got even more reasons to want to stay."

"I told you," Luther said, kissing him softly. "I understand deployment. As long as I get those late-night calls and texts, I'm perfectly happy. And Violet is super supportive of this thing we have going. She said she's willing to stay with Mila overnight anytime she's off work, so think about it."

Doug's eyes rolled back. "All night to use a Marine? Could I even handle it?"

"I don't know," Luther said with a sigh. "Guess we'll have to see."

"God, please? I want you."

Luther kissed him once more with those deep tongue sweeps that promised to fulfill all the Dougish Desires he could possibly dream up. This man, this honorable, complex, wonderful man, made his heart spill over. If they could find a way to make this work, Doug might just have to rethink his nomadic ways. Or, perhaps he could see some of those places on his bucket list with Luther…and Mila.

"Go get pretty for me. I can't wait to see those legs in fishnets." He nibbled on Doug's lip before stepping back. "I'm going to go find my girls."

Doug didn't trust himself to speak, so he waved. Speaking might lead to begging, might lead to confessions he wasn't ready to make. Instead, he marched across the yard, up the steps, and into his room, where he found his band members getting dressed. Correction, they were half dressed because they'd been spying on Doug and Luther.

"If you're done sucking face with that DILF, I'd love your help with my makeup."

"DILF?" He rolled his eyes at Barb. "You don't even like dick."

"Yeah, but a girl can appreciate a fine specimen."

"I bet he wants to suck more than his face," Monica said.

Sunny started making kissing sounds and things devolved from there, exactly as they should before they put on an in-your-face performance.

NINE

Luther

"There you are," he said as he rejoined Violet and Mila next to the food truck. "Have you ordered yet?"

"Daddy, can we go to the book bus first, please? I want to look at the books."

"You know I will never say no to books," he said to her. "Lead on."

"Hey, you okay?" Violet asked.

He grinned and rubbed his chest. "Real good. I might need your help, though. Soon. With a discussion."

She frowned, but then she nodded. "You got it. I'm going to go grab us some chairs for the show. You want to be front and center?" She winked at him. "You guys bring back some teriyaki bowls when you come. I'm starving."

"Copy that."

Mila took his hand and started to drag him toward the

rainbow-colored bus, but then she looked at his cane and she slowed down, settling for doing some sort of skipping, twisting dance instead. As they got closer, Mila read the words painted on the side.

"Hook's Traveling Book Nook. Daddy, is it their job to ride around with books all the time?"

"Sounds like a pretty awesome job." Luther grinned. There were two older women dressed as brightly as the bus sitting on camp chairs next to the bus, knitting.

Mila stepped behind him as they approached.

"Well, hello there! Welcome to Hook's Book Nook! What kind of stories do you like to read?" One of the ladies pulled her glasses down her nose and looked at Mila.

Mila stared at her with wide eyes and didn't answer.

"I love fairy books," Luther finally said. "And dragons. Basically any animals."

The other woman chuckled and set down her knitting. "I think we have just what you're looking for."

"You hear that?" Luther stage-whispered to Mila. "They have fairies and dragons. And animals."

Mila giggled and followed the woman up the steps into the bus, but she tightened her grip on Luther's hand. He felt her excitement as she trembled with joy at the sight of all the books, which were organized by age rather than genre.

"Let me guess," the woman said. "You're in second grade?"

Mila's eyes went wide. "How did you know?" she whispered in awe.

The woman shrugged. "I've got an eye for that sort of thing. So, here are the shelves where I think we'll find what your...dad is looking for." She winked at Luther, who gave her a subtle thumbs up.

But instead of perusing the shelves the woman had shown her, Mila was drawn to a basket with some picture books inside. Luther watched as she knelt down in front of it and plucked a book with the utmost care, as if she were removing a priceless jewel from a display case. Luther couldn't see the book's title so he moved behind her.

"*Pringle and Finn, The Pengrooms.* That's cute."

Mila hugged it to her chest and walked down the aisle to the benches and sat down with the book.

Luther shared a look with the woman, both of their eyebrows raised. He hobbled down the aisle of the bus, hunching slightly to avoid smacking his head. He lowered himself to the bench next to her, making the minimum old-man noises possible, but the bench was low. He wasn't exactly sure how he was going to get up.

"You like that one, sweetheart?"

She nodded and spoke in the tiny voice she'd used when she first came to live with him. "I used to have this book. I wasn't allowed to take it with me when I left."

Luther's heart nearly broke, remembering how frightened she was that day, how she'd had to sleep with the lights on for days, how she wouldn't let Terry D'actyl out of her sight.

"I'm sorry," he said, putting a hand on her back. "Books are really important. I'm sorry I haven't taken you to the library more, or the bookstore. I forget how much I loved books at your age."

She looked up at him. "This one was special. I got it from my old school for getting good attendance."

"Can you read it to me?" Luther asked, not trusting himself to speak.

She opened the book and started telling the story of a pair of penguins who made special wedding cakes for their animal friends, until finally, they had a wedding for themselves in their backyard. Luther's breath grew shaky as she got to the end of the story.

"I love when you read to me," he said to her. "That was a nice story."

"I like reading stories about people who love each other."

"Me, too," Luther admitted, although most of the books he read were fantasy, they weren't really love books. "What do you like about them?"

She ran her fingers over the picture of the penguins cuddled together in a chair at the end of the story, their rainbow bow ties on the floor. "I like it when people who love each other get to be together, be a family. My older brother had to leave because our mom wouldn't let him be with his boyfriend. They loved each other a lot."

Luther's face got hot, and he clutched the top of his cane tightly. This was the most she'd ever talked about her family. He'd known there had been neglect and abuse with one of Mila's siblings, and that her mother had dumped her on an elderly parent with dementia and split.

"That must have made you sad," he finally said.

She nodded and continued to trace the penguins on the page. "He took care of me. He told me when two people love each other, it doesn't matter if they're boys or girls."

"I think your brother is pretty smart," Luther said, his voice cracking. This conversation was delicate and he wanted to do it just right. "Do you think he was right?"

She looked up at him with big eyes and nodded vigorously. "As long as people love each other and are kind to each other."

He took in a deep breath, ready to step off the ledge. "Mila, sweetheart, you know that I'm gay? That someday I may have my own groom?"

She nodded. "I heard you and Miss Vanessa talking about it before. Do you love somebody?"

"I think so," he said. "But no matter what, you know you're always going to be my family, right? No matter who else comes into our lives?"

"Yes, Daddy. We're family."

Luther exhaled and put his arm around her, pulling her in for a hug and kissing the top of her head. "You're the smartest girl I know," he said. This was a big enough revelation for the day, but it opened the door to other conversations. He would find a way to talk to her about Doug, and then, maybe they could spend some time together. Maybe he really could make it work, being her dad and being Doug's person.

That scenario gave Luther hope.

"Did you want to look at some more books?" he asked, thinking Violet would start texting him soon if he didn't feed her.

She held the book to her chest. "Can I have this one?" she whispered. "Can I use my allowance money to buy it?"

"Sweetheart, I told you. Daddy will always let you have books. You save your allowance money for something else, okay?"

She grinned. "Thank you, Daddy. I love you."

Well, there went the waterworks. Luther had asked Miss Vanessa at their last meeting what to do about *I love yous*. He wasn't sure whether it was okay, whether it would make Mila feel uncomfortable if he said it, but Miss Vanessa told him absolutely he could say it to her.

"No matter what happens with her placement, you will always have a bond with her, and I get the sense that she didn't hear it much at her home. Kids need to know they're loved."

Luther fully agreed. He'd found that familial love with Violet early on and that had been all he needed to make it through. He'd felt that love for Bunker and his teammates, and that made the hard times bearable. He wanted to be that person for Mila, and to hear her say it, made his hard times more bearable too.

"I love you, too, sweetheart. I'm so glad you're my family."

They pressed their foreheads together and he squeezed his eyes shut to hopefully keep the tears from falling.

"Dear, if you like that book, I think I have some other books you might like, too. Would you like to come look?" The kind old woman stood there smiling at them, her eyes a little shiny too. "I can hold on to that one for you, if you like, until you're done looking.

Mila looked to Luther and he nodded. "I'll hang on to it. Go ahead, Mila. Take your time."

He appreciated the time to flip through the book again and smile at the little penguins and their rainbow bow ties, spreading love through sweets all through the land.

Just like Doug.

Maybe you can have it all. He wouldn't have his beloved Marine Corps, but he had a daughter to love, a sister at his back, and a man who made him feel ten feet tall.

His thoughts traveled to Oscar. Obviously someone had spent a lot of time with that dog, and somehow he'd ended up without a home. Luther hoped it wasn't because he'd been discarded, and it also bothered him to think his owner might have passed away, and he'd had no one to take on his dog.

Luther had no business thinking about adding a pet to his mix right now, but something in that dog's demeanor called to him...and *man* it felt good to have a dog at his side, even if it had only been for a few minutes.

Maybe he could see if Dinah wanted him to work with Oscar a little more. Spending some time with the dog could help him come out of his shell and make him appear more attractive to folks looking to adopt. He'd had a pretty shaggy coat and a little gray around his muzzle, so he'd definitely seen some mileage. Luther worried the dog might have medical needs that would go beyond his meager ability to pay.

No soldier left behind.

Luther's heart hurt thinking this dog very well may have

been in service to a human being, and as such, he deserved better than to live out his days alone in a kennel.

"Daddy! Come look."

She had a book in her hands and was bouncing on her toes. When he managed to get to standing and made his way to her side, she turned the book around—and his heart thudded hard in his chest.

"He looks like your dog, Bunker."

The book was *Max*. He remembered seeing ads for a movie version. "He sure does," Luther said, his throat tight.

"He's a military dog, just like Bunker was."

One afternoon, he'd been hanging up her artwork after her second week at camp, and she came wandering in his room. She'd asked about his pictures, and they'd spent the afternoon talking about his job as a soldier and about Bunker. She'd wanted to know everything, but there were things an eight-year-old didn't need to know about the work he'd done.

"That book sure is popular with young folks," the lady said. "It should be okay for her reading level. She showed me some of the books she's read at school, and I think it's a good fit."

Luther agreed, but he also needed to mentally prepare himself for the questions she'd have after reading it.

"We could read it together, Daddy."

"Okay, okay," he said. If he didn't get out of that bus he was going to sweat through his shirt and cry his damn eyes out. He reached for his wallet and the lady held up her hands.

"Our books come from donations. They've all been read and loved by someone previously. If you wish to make a donation, there's a box and a QR code on the side of the bus."

Luther nodded, and he handed the penguin book back to Mila. "Say thank you, sweetheart."

Mila hugged the books to her chest and gave the woman a

big smile. "Thank you for the books. I will love them very much."

The lady held out a fist and Mila bumped it with hers, letting out a little giggle, then she scampered out of the bus.

"You all right there, soldier?" the woman asked kindly.

"Yes, ma'am. Be even better if you have a tissue."

She chuckled and held out a box. "I hope I didn't pry too much."

He shook his head as he wiped at his eyes and nose. "Not at all. She's my foster daughter, so every moment like this is a win, you know? Thank you for being part of that today."

She gave a funny curtsy and laughed. "You're welcome."

At that moment, a squeal of feedback ripped through the air, and Mila came running back up the stairs.

"Hurry, Daddy. Doug is going to play!" And then she was gone again.

That was enough to get Luther moving. He thanked the lady once more and made his way gingerly down the steps of the bus, grateful he'd brought his cane. His legs had felt like they weighed a hundred fifty pounds each this morning, but thankfully the pain hadn't been too bad. He hadn't wanted to miss seeing Doug, and after this breakthrough with Mila, he was even more grateful they'd come.

The band started playing a Clash tune that he recognized, and Mila once more tried not to drag him up the path to where the stage area was located.

"Wait, we gotta get food for Auntie Violet."

Mila did not seem happy about that, but she stood impatiently by as he ordered them each bowls and drinks. One of the women sang the first song, and when it finished, another feminine voice sang a Hole song he remembered well.

They'd just gotten their food when the third song started, and this time a deep voice rang out, singing "I Wanna Be Your Dog" by the Stooges. He quickened his pace, letting go of

Mila's hand so she could run for Auntie Violet. He made it around the corner of the house and the stage came into view. Luther nearly dropped the food.

Doug was front and center on the stage wearing an open black vest with patches on it and no shirt, black hot pants, and fishnets that hugged his gorgeous legs all the way down to the tops of his platform boots. *Jesus.* Luther's mouth watered at the sight. He managed to make it to Violet, who had grabbed chairs on the outside aisle near the front, but no one was sitting. Mila was jumping and dancing with some of the other kids in front of the stage, and Violet was bobbing her head to the beat.

"Your man wears the shit out of those hot pants," she yelled into Luther's ear.

"You think?" he said, his face hot. Goddamn, he hadn't prepared himself for how fucking sexy his man would be playing guitar and singing his heart out, his black-lipsticked lips pressed to the microphone. He looked up and caught Luther's gaze, and he smiled that same smile he'd had when he'd gone down on Luther the first time.

This was not going to stay a family show for long if Luther didn't get his libido in check.

Doug was captivating to watch onstage. All that energy, all that charisma, he let it all out. He had that chameleonic type of voice that could sing just about anything, and he really did. The members of the band took turns, but Doug belted out tunes from The Misfits, Rise Against, and the Ramones, as well as a lovely rendition of The Smiths' "There Is A Light," which, despite its morbid lyrics, Luther took as quite a romantic proclamation, especially since Doug's eyes were on him for most of the song. He was magnetic, sensual, and Luther felt like he was levitating. Today, he'd had an overdose of emotions, and by the time Doug finished the tune, Luther had to sit down, though he worried he might not be able to get back up.

The band played a riotous version of "Seven Nation Army" by the White Stripes to wrap up their set and everyone jumped to their feet to sing along. Luther sat back and closed his eyes, absorbing the energy around him, the sounds of Mila and Violet laughing above the other crowd noises, and the cool breeze of the fall evening.

This might have been the closest to heaven he'd ever been.

"Hey, you okay, LuLu?" Violet asked, her hand gentle on his shoulder.

He opened his eyes as folks around them were packing up their stuff to leave. The band members were mingling with the crowd, and Mila was frowning at him.

"Daddy, how did you fall asleep?"

He made a show of looking at his Apple watch and frowned. "Because it's past my bedtime. Which means it's past yours too."

She rolled her eyes, giving him a glimpse of teenage-hood to come, and he laughed.

"Let's go say goodbye to Doug and Dinah and hit the road," Luther said, accepting Violet's help to get to his feet."

"Actually, Mila and I decided that she and I are going to have a sleepover and do facials tonight, since you and Doug have work to do." Violet's eyebrows went way up, her expression letting him know this was not up for discussion.

"Yeah. Work." He frowned, looking for Doug. "Does... Doug know about us working?"

"Oh yes," she said. "I talked to him earlier. He said he wanted you to stick around and help him with the thing."

Bless his sister and her conniving ways. He could barely stand, but if he could hold out for a few more minutes, he might get to actually spend a whole night with Doug.

"But I'll miss out on all the fun," he said, winking at Violet.

"It's okay for you to miss facials, Daddy," Mila assured him. "You can make me pancakes for breakfast."

Violet snorted and gave him a little shrug as she placed a hand on the girl's shoulder. "Or, we could go get donuts," she stage-whispered to Mila.

Mila was definitely like her dad, she had a bit of a sweet tooth. She turned to him and patted his arm. "Yeah, Daddy, you should stay working with Doug. Just come home when you're done, okay?" She hugged him around his waist, and then grabbed Violet's hand. "Good night, Daddy. See you tomorrow."

Violet waved as the two of them did their twisty skip dance down the path to where they'd parked Violet's car.

"You stayed," Doug said, wrapping his arms around Luther's waist from behind. "I was hoping Violet would talk you into it."

Luther placed his hand over Doug's and sighed. "I wasn't given a choice. The deal was cemented when she promised Mila donuts in the morning."

Doug nibbled on Luther's earlobe, and he had to steady himself with his cane.

"You're so much sweeter than donuts," he whispered into Luther's ear.

He turned and pulled Doug close.

"Be careful, I'm sweaty."

"You know I like sweaty."

Doug grinned at him. "You like the show?"

"You know I did."

Doug sighed. "So, are you ready to...work?"

"You know it. No way I'm letting you take those stockings off by yourself."

Doug's expression grew serious as he stepped back. "I'm so glad you came."

Luther was tempted to make a lewd comment, but something had shifted. Doug really was worried, even after their conversation. Luther couldn't have that.

"Wouldn't have missed it, but I'm fading fast. Any chance we can get started?"

Doug pulled him toward the house. "Let's do it. The girls are finishing breaking down the equipment, and I told Dinah I'd be in charge of cleanup in the morning. Let's get you to bed."

"Copy that."

Luther was introduced to several people—he was sure he'd have to ask Doug for their names again later—and then they made their way into the house, where he waved to Dinah.

"I promise I'll make proper introductions when you're not ready to drop," Doug said. "Thankfully my room is downstairs. It's just through here."

Doug led Luther through a living room and down another hallway toward the back of the house. The place was old but sturdy, and someone had added on to it several times over the years. The section he and Doug were headed toward looked older than the front.

"I've got a bedroom and an office back here, plus my own bathroom."

Luther exhaled in relief when they passed through a door and he spotted Doug's bed. He wouldn't have cared if it was a cot at this point. He just needed to get horizontal.

"You look like you're going to drop," Doug said, sitting Luther on the bed. He bent down and unlaced Luther's boots, gently pulling them and his socks off. "You need the bathroom?"

Luther wordlessly pulled Doug close and wrapped his

arms around his torso, resting his head on his chest. "I just need you."

Doug smiled and bent down to kiss him. "Me too. Let's get you undressed and in bed. I'll take a quick shower and join you, okay?"

Luther complained about missing out on fishnet stocking removal duty and supervising shower activities, but Luther allowed Doug to get his jeans off and pull off his shirt. Doug lifted his legs onto the bed, and Luther didn't even growl about being able to do it his damn self. The bed was unbelievably soft and as soon as his head hit the pillow, he could barely keep his eyes open. Well, he managed to keep one eye open to watch Doug begin to undress, but once the hot pants were off, Luther lost the battle.

He woke sometime before dawn and tried not to wake Doug as he got to his feet, held back the old-man noises, and was grateful for whoever put a nightlight in the bathroom so he didn't stumble and fall in the dark. He did his business and crawled gingerly back into bed with Doug.

"Don't say it's morning," Doug said, wrapping himself around Luther. "I haven't gotten to use a Marine yet."

Luther brushed his hair back and kissed his forehead. "Then get on up here and use this Marine."

Thank the powers that be that Doug was not only strong but incredibly coordinated. He straddled Luther's hips and whispered sweet nothings as he used his fingers to prepare his entrance for Luther. He managed to roll a condom onto his Marine and lowered himself carefully, taking all of Luther inside him without putting any weight on his pelvis.

"You're so fucking good," Luther said, as Doug took care of them both. He moved at an achingly slow pace, only trembling from the sensation, not from the effort of supporting himself. Luther stroked him in time with his movements as they stared into each other's eyes.

"You *feel* so fucking good," Doug whispered back, bending down to kiss Luther deeply. "So good, I'm going to come too soon, baby. I'm sorry, you're hitting my fucking prostate so good...*fuck*."

Luther held his face and forced Doug to look at him. "No sorry. Take what you need, beautiful. Ride me. Get yourself off. I can take it."

Doug's eyes went wide for a moment, and then he moved with a little more determination, though not as much as Luther knew he could. He squeezed Doug's thick thighs and let his head fall back. His eyes closed, and he lost himself in Doug's body, the heat and the pressure working in tandem to pull forth the mother of all orgasms from his very soul.

He cried out, the sensation so intense he had a moment of fear that his body was going to quit, but then Doug's muscles clamped down on him, and Luther felt Doug's warmth coat his chest. It was enough to clear his mind of worry and allow him to relax enough for his own release to barrel through him.

"Fuck, *Doug*," he cried, and then his heart was pounding so hard he could barely catch his breath. Doug pulled off of him carefully and disposed of the condom. Doug used a washcloth to clean them both up, and then he lay back down beside Luther, caressing his chest as Luther fought to slow his breathing down.

"Are you okay?" Doug asked him ,and Luther chuckled.

"I think so? Damn. That was—"

"Divine, oh my God." Doug pressed his forehead to Luther's. "Did I hurt you? I tried not to."

"You were perfect," Luther said, running his thumb over Doug's lip. "Best sleepover ever. Way better than facials."

Doug fell back on the bed cackling, then he kicked at Luther's leg. "I can't believe you."

"What? It was!"

Doug shook his head and pushed up on his elbow. "I was worried there for a minute."

Luther sighed. "Me too. I need to work on my cardio, I guess. Told you, I'm an old man. You're trying to make me one of those ancient bazillionaires who croak in bed having sex with their hot young things."

"I mean, it's a helluva way to go," Doug said, and it was Luther's turn to kick at his leg. "I'm kidding. Gosh. I want to keep you around long enough to enjoy those bazillions. Plus, you're right, it's handy to have a Marine around for my personal use. I could get accustomed to this."

"Do. Do get used to it," Luther said, cutting through the banter. "I had a conversation with Mila. It's a long story, but she's...she knows I'm gay, and she understands."

Doug blew out a breath. "That's really good news."

"Yeah," Luther said. "I want us to... Do you want to—"

"I want to. Let's make this happen."

Part Four
Winter Solstice

TEN

D^{oug}

"You ready, buddy?"

Doug looked at Oscar in the mirror as he put the finishing touches on his makeup. The fluffy grouch's ears perked up and he cocked his head to the side.

"It's a big night for both of us, man. We gotta look good."

Oscar's head tilted the other way, and Doug smiled.

They'd had a wildly successful day at the Treasure Island market, the last one of the year. In addition to their usual fare, Doug had made photo ornaments to sell, baking them with clay, painting some and leaving others for families to decorate. He offered personalization and his wrist had cramped from all the pet names he'd written on them.

Luther had spent the past two months using ornament-size pieces of wood and decorated them with traditional

Christmas, Pagan, and Jewish symbols for folks to buy as gifts, and they'd been a huge hit. Luther had decided for the spring, he was going to cut back on doing the art and markets so he could save energy for his job at Mila's school and for spending time with her, Violet, and Doug.

If all went well tonight, Luther wouldn't have to worry about working so hard for extra money anyway.

"Hey, you guys almost ready?" Dinah asked, peeking in his bedroom door.

"Almost. I'm trying to prepare Oscar, to impart upon him the importance of tonight. I'm not sure he understands the weight of this momentous occasion."

Dinah sat on his bed next to Oscar and put a hand on his back. "You're such a drama llama, Doug. It's going to be great. Everything is going to work out perfect."

He blew out a breath and shook out his hands. He straightened his sleeveless black tuxedo t-shirt and smoothed down his black utility kilt, which had raised velvet skulls on the material. He'd polished his Dr. Martens to be sure they had a nice shine on them. He'd wanted to look perfect.

"It's a big step."

Dinah smiled. "You're ready. It's going to be great. Marianne will be there with the camera to catch all the action, all right?"

Doug turned and walked over to the bed, putting his hand on Oscar's head. The big oaf rubbed his head on Doug's hand and made an old-man noise that sounded remarkably like Luther.

"Okay. Let's get this over with. Here, buddy. The piece de resistance."

He pulled out a black bow tie with white skulls on it and fastened it around Oscar's neck, the dog allowing him to do whatever at this point. He'd mastered bath time, and Oscar even let him trim his nails as long as he put peanut butter on his forehead for the dog to lick off. They'd come a long way, and Doug had worked hard to earn his trust. It was all thanks to Luther.

He fastened Oscar's leash to his collar, and Dinah laughed. "Remember the first time you tried to do that?"

The morning after the first night Luther stayed with Doug, they'd talked about Oscar. Luther had expressed his concern for the dog and his desire to do right by the guy. Doug had come up with a brilliant plan.

"Why don't you teach *me*, and I'll foster him."

Luther's eyes had gone wide. "Have you ever had a dog before?"

Doug shrugged and deadpanned, "My mom had a shih tzu when I was a kid. Same thing, right? That thing hated me."

Luther had shaken his head. "Honey, a German shepherd is in an entirely different category than—"

"I get it," Doug said. "That's why it's good you'll be there to help me. We can co-parent. It'll be good practice."

Luther's eyes brightened when he realized what Doug was saying. If they were going to make this relationship work, the ultimate goal was that Doug would join Luther's little family. If he had his own ward, then they'd be a truly blended family.

"Besides," Doug had said. "I bet you Mila will be totally onboard if I come with a dog as part of the package."

Luther had scoffed at him, but Doug insisted. "It'll be good for all of us, baby. I'm going to need all the training I can get if I'm adopting an old grouch, a dog, *and* preparing to help raise a pre-teen."

"Ha ha." Then Luther sighed. "We're going to need a lot more than a rudimentary knowledge of German commands to get through the latter."

So each Sunday for the next month, Luther had come over

to the farm and they'd spent time working with Oscar. Doug practiced what they learned every day in between and after the second week, Oscar finally gave up pretenses and his aloof attitude. Doug had assured him that resistance was futile. Oscar *would* love him. There was no fighting it. Luther always said confidence was the key, so Doug was determined it would be true.

Now the two were inseparable.

The next step was to bring Mila out for the training sessions, and this time Doug taught Mila how to handle Oscar while Luther supervised. The dog had been a little unsure of her at first, and she'd had to be instructed not to run or skip around him. She listened so well to both Doug and Luther that the lessons went smoothly from then on.

In the meantime, Doug began having family dinners with them once a week. He and Mila would spend time singing and dancing afterward, or he'd let her do his makeup, always praising her creations no matter how interesting they looked. They'd celebrated Thanksgiving together, Violet's birthday, and they'd gone to the theater to see the stage performance of *Beetlejuice*, which Mila had gone bonkers over.

Tonight was the winter solstice, and Doug felt it was the perfect time to show his gratitude and celebrate all the good times to come. It would be the longest night of the year, and each night after would bring them further into the light. He wanted to make a commitment before his friends and his new family to face this change of seasons, and all of those to come, together.

It had been Dinah's idea to have an adoption ceremony for Oscar since they'd all invested so much into his rehabilitation. It was tradition to celebrate the solstice with a bonfire, and the Shaw sisters had wanted to do it safely, so they'd spent the past week building a secure fire pit. They'd prepared a vegan feast—

Doug was happy to go without meat for this special occasion—and all that was left was for their guests to arrive.

"Hey twerp," his cousin Marianne said as she stuck her head in. "I see the truck heading up the drive. You ready?"

"Ready as I'll ever be."

The sisters, Doug's family—including Marianne's parents—and Doug with Oscar in tow headed out to the fire pit circle to wait for Luther, Violet and Mila to join them. Luther was moving slow tonight because of the long day at the market. Doug looked forward to taking care of him later...and from now on.

"Don't you two look handsome," Violet said, reaching him first and hugging him. She whispered in his ear, "You ready?"

Doug kissed her cheek. "So ready."

Violet had become one of Doug's favorite people in the whole world. Not only was she a great auntie to Mila, taking a very active part in her niece's life, but she was also steadfast in her support of Luther. She'd been very welcoming of Doug into their lives, and she was totally onboard with tonight's agenda.

"Put 'er there, partner," Doug said to Mila as he held out a hand for her to shake. They'd been on this weird cowboy kick after watching the entire *Toy Story* series together. Mila shook his hand up and down and then giggled. She held out her hand to Oscar, and when he nuzzled it, she stood closer to him and patted his back. She was so good.

Luther leaned over and kissed his cheek. "You look dashing," he whispered in Doug's ear.

Doug's heart skipped around for a second as he smiled at Luther. He'd come to love everything about this man, and his soft smile tonight, combined with the sparkle of mischief in his eyes over the part of tonight's ceremony they'd planned together, nearly overwhelmed him. Dinah shushed everyone, and Doug gave Luther's hand a squeeze.

"Welcome everyone," Dinah said. "Let's all take a seat by the fire and Cecily will get things started for us."

Cecily was the quietest of the Shaw sisters. Doug loved sharing space with her in the kitchen while she worked on her creations and Doug cooked for the family. He loved her dedication to keeping the farm operational and her devotion to her animals.

As she stood and held up a wand lighter, she smiled at those gathered.

"We're glad you all could be here to celebrate the changing of the seasons with us. From here, the days will become longer and with each moment, we'll be closer to the light. Tonight is Yule, and we are grateful to all be here together in the light. Let the fire warm us, and let our love for each other sustain us as we move closer to the sun and the rebirth of Spring."

"Blessed be," Doug murmured along with his housemates. His aunt and uncle whispered to each other but his uncle Mason, bless him, he just smiled and nodded at the pagan flavor of this gathering.

Cecily lit the kindling, and Dinah and Trudy handed out glasses of sparkling cider to everyone. The flames grew to a nice warm fire, the perfect size for them to enjoy with no fear of it spreading. They had shovels and buckets of water on hand just in case. On the California hillsides, it was crucial to have safety in mind at all times.

"Tonight, we would like to make a toast to family, to the one we're born into, and the one we choose."

They all held up their plastic flutes and toasted folks next to each other. Doug and Luther peered at each other over their drinks. Mila tugged on Luther's sweater.

"This is okay for me to drink too?"

He smiled at her. "It's apple juice with bubbles, sweetheart. Go ahead."

She slurped hers down and her eyes went wide. "It tickles my nose," she said, giggling with Violet.

Dinah set her cup down and smiled at Doug. "We have so much to celebrate tonight. It's been a banner year for Goth Dog Rescue, and the farm side, under Cecily's care, is finally operating in the black. We've also added to our family, and that's honestly my favorite part. I want to thank Doug Cross for being an awesome housemate, business partner, and as of today, new dad. Ladies and gentleman, Doug has decided to adopt Oscar, and tonight we're making it official."

There were applause all around, but Doug was most concerned with Mila's reaction. Her eyes were big and she patted Oscar's back.

"Way to go, buddy," she said to him. He nosed her cheek then went back to panting happily next to Doug.

But then Mila's smile started to slip a little, and she looked down at the ground.

It was time for the next phase of the evening.

"Thank you, everyone," Doug began. "I'm so grateful to have met Oscar and that, with Luther's guiding hand, I've learned how to be the right kind of dad for him. We'll obviously have to work hard at it, but learning with him has been one of the most rewarding things I've ever done. I want to thank Dinah for seeing in him a special grumpy guy who just needed a little sunshine to make him happy."

Dinah brought over a certificate she'd made, and she had Doug hold it while Marianne took pictures of them together. Everyone clapped, and then Doug cleared his throat and gave Luther the signal.

"Thanks, everyone, for inviting my family to join in the celebration," Luther began. "For a couple of kids who didn't have families, it's very special for Violet and me to be welcomed by folks like you."

Everyone smiled, and then Luther used his cane to lower himself to one knee beside Mila. There was a murmur of concern as he winced a little, but he was all smiles when he took Mila's hands in his. Her eyes were large as saucers as she looked around at everyone then back at him.

"Our family expanded a little over a year ago when Mila came into my life, and it's changed everything for the better." She smiled but it was hesitant, and Doug could tell by Luther's expression, it was about to get silly. "I'm now a jazz aficionado, I can braid hair like nobody's business, and I've perfected my pancake game." She giggled, but Doug could see she was still confused.

"When you find the right person to bring into your family, you want to make it official. So Mila, I wanted to know if you'd like to be my daughter for good? It's your decision whether or not we begin the adoption process, and you can talk to Miss Vanessa about it if you're not sure—"

She threw her arms around his neck and burst into tears. He grunted as she nearly knocked him over. Everyone in the circle wiped at their leaking eyes.

"Hang on now, sweetheart, I have something for you."

But Mila was sobbing and wouldn't let him go. He closed his eyes and took a moment to breathe. Doug knew Luther had been concerned that Mila might not be sure about going forward with adoption, but Doug thought her reaction meant it was safe to assume Luther got the answer he'd hoped for. Once she'd settled down, he reached into his pocket and pulled out a jewelry box.

"You don't have to answer now," Luther said to her, but she reached out and squished his cheeks in her hands.

"Yes, please! I want to be adopted like Oscar."

Everyone in the circle was now full-blown sobbing,

including Doug. It was exactly the reaction he'd hoped she'd have.

"Here, sweetheart. I had this made for you." Luther opened the box, and Doug held his breath. They'd gone together to pick out a locket for her. On the front it was engraved with "Mila" and on the back it said "Sorenson." He'd put a picture of himself and Violet in one side and left the other open for her to decide. Luther put it around her neck and then opened it up to show her the inside.

Mila frowned. "Who goes on this side?"

Luther looked up at Doug and his smile fell. He moved Mila to his side and whispered for her to hold on to his cane for a second.

She got a big smile on her face, her eyes went wide, and she bounced on her feet.

Luther dug in his other pocket and brought out another box.

"I was hoping we could add one more person to our family tonight." He reached for Doug's hand, and the faintest wince crossed his face.

"Luther, you need to get up right now," Doug whispered to him, his chest so tight he didn't think he could get in another breath.

"I will when I have your answer. Doug, will you join my—*our*—family?"

Mila and Violet hugged each other then clapped their hands. *Aha.* Apparently they were in on this part.

"You beat me to it, baby. I was going to ask you the same thing. See?"

Doug bent down and whispered a command to Oscar. He put up his right paw, and Doug sat a ring box on top of it. They'd been practicing this trick for days, and he wasn't sure if Oscar would perform under pressure.

"Now that's just showing off," Luther said through gritted

teeth as though he wasn't sure if the pain or his emotions would overwhelm him first. He reached for the box and patted Oscar on the head. Then he gave Doug a pained look. "Help me up?"

The group all burst into cheers around them. Doug reached for Luther's hand and helped him to stand, which elicited all kinds of old-man noises. Mila went to his other side and held his arm, then put his cane in his hand.

"Well what do you say, Daddy? Are you going to marry Doug or what?"

Luther laughed at her, but he was out of breath. His little stunt had not been a good idea.

"Do you need to sit?" Doug asked, moving closer to support him better, and Luther thankfully allowed Doug and Mila to lead him over to a sturdy chair. Violet held it steady while Doug lowered him to a sitting position.

Dinah announced that the food was ready. "How about we leave the happy family to have a moment to themselves."

She winked at Doug, and he mouthed "thank you."

"Thank you, and yeah, sweetheart. I'm going to marry him. I'm gonna need *all* of you to carry me around when my legs completely give out."

Violet laughed and messed up his hair.

"Good," she said. "I could use all the help I can get to keep you in line."

"And Oscar, Daddy. He'll help you too. And that means I get a brother! I think I'll put a picture of Oscar in the other side of my locket."

"I see where I rank," Doug muttered only loud enough for Luther to hear. He wanted Mila to be happy above all, and Oscar was a pretty cool dog for a grouch.

Luther kissed her cheek. "Why don't you and Violet go and get your food, okay? I'll see you in a minute."

"Good, I'm starving," she said, grabbing Violet's hand.

Doug was pleased as punch that she'd become much more outgoing around everyone. They were going to have so much fun.

Once they were gone, Luther pulled Doug in for a tight hug, and he exhaled a shaky breath. He held on for several long minutes, and when he let go, Doug grabbed a chair and slid it over next to him.

"I thought about being all romantic about this proposal," Luther said, holding Doug's hands, "but I wanted Mila to be a part of it. She loves you, Doug. She talks about you all the time. And it'll be a process, if you say yes and you want to get married. Steps we have to take, and then with the adoption, there will be home visits...I understand if it's too much—"

"Luther, I already contacted DSS to ask about the classes, and I've registered for CPR and first-aid classes next month. If you really want me to be part of your family, I'm all in."

Luther stared at him for several beats without speaking. He shook his head finally and sighed. "Did you even imagine when we met all those months ago—"

"When you fell out of your trailer—"

"And you caught me, that we'd be here?"

Doug cupped Luther's cheek. "I had your back then, and I want to have it from now on. I'm so in love with you, Luther Sorenson. Can we get married?"

Luther exhaled and his eyes filled with tears. "We most certainly can."

The rest of the evening was full of stories, music, snacks, and laughter so hearty it gave Doug a belly ache. At the end of the night, Luther started yawning, and Violet told him she'd take Mila home.

"But I want us to go home together," he said.

"You're barely going to make it to Doug's room. Besides, the two of you have plans to make...like when he's moving in."

Luther squeezed Violet's hand and smiled at her. "I love you, sis."

"Me too, LuLu. Mila, come kiss Daddy. It's time for us to go home."

But Mila and Oscar had curled up together on a lounge chair and were fast asleep.

"Why don't you all stay," Doug said. "I've got a pull-out couch in my office for Mila and there's a spare room upstairs for you, Violet. I'd feel better if we were all together tonight."

Violet pressed her lips together, and Doug worried he'd said the wrong thing. He started to apologize when she threw her arms around him.

"Thank you," she whispered. "I didn't know how much I needed to hear that."

"You got it, sister. Let's get these two inside."

Doug took one last look at the fire and breathed in the aromatic smoke from the incense Cecily had thrown into it. Tomorrow would be a little brighter, surrounded by his new family, with the most wonderful man by his side.

Even if he made old-man noises.

"I can do it myself," Luther grumbled as Violet tried to help him up.

"Good, you big lug."

Doug bent down and scooped up Mila. She stirred and opened one eye.

"Do I get to call you daddy too?"

Doug's chest filled with warmth, and he smiled at her, kissing her forehead. "You could. Or maybe we can come up with something fun, like Daddy-o or Big Papa."

"Lord, we've created a monster," Luther said as he put a hand on Doug's back. He whistled for Oscar, who trotted alongside them as they all made their way into the house.

"Like Dr. Frank-n-Furter," Doug said to Luther, his eyes wide, his eyebrows waggling.

"You mean *Rocky Horror Picture Show*? I like that movie."

They all stopped and peered at the sleepy girl.

"Excuse me?" Luther said sternly.

Her eyes got big. "It was my brother's favorite movie. He used to go see it at the theaters with his boyfriend."

Luther exhaled. "Oh. Well."

Mila yawned and her eyes drifted closed, but she started to sing something with slurred words. *"It's just a jump to the left."*

Violet snorted, and Doug had a hard time keeping it together. Violet and Luther pulled out the sofa bed and Doug pointed to the closet for pillows and blankets. Once they had Mila tucked in, Oscar jumped onto the bed and curled up to her back, looking at Luther as if he dared him to try to make him move.

Luther let out a sigh. "I've lost all parental control."

Violet kissed his cheek. "Control is an illusion. Doug? Show me where the spare room is?"

Doug smiled at Luther and said, "I'll be right back, old man."

Luther waved and lowered himself to the bed in Doug's room, which gave him a direct line of sight to the sofa bed in the alcove outside Doug's door.

Once Doug had Violet settled, he crept down the stairs quietly. He found Luther passed out on the bed, his feet still on the floor.

Doug smiled, looking between father and daughter. His new family. He had no qualms about taking care of both of them for the rest of his life. It was amazing what the change of seasons could bring. In his case, he'd received the love of a wonderful man, the trust of a sweet little girl, a kick-ass new sister, and the companionship of an ornery dog.

Who could ask for anything more?

. . .

Stay Tuned for more...

Please be sure to check out all the books in the Once Upon a Holiday Story Multi-author Series:

Once Upon a Second Chance by Davidson King
    Once Upon a Mistletoe Kiss by Sammi Cee
    Once Upon a Holiday Vacation by Annabella Michaels
    Once Upon a Lullaby Lane by K. York
    Once Upon a Christmas Con by Skylar M. Cates
    Once Upon a Christmas Song by Mary Calmes
    Once Upon a Yuletide Romance by R.J. Peterson
    Once Upon a Goth Dog Solstice by RL Merrill

If you'd like to read the Goth Dog Rescue origin story, check out *Pinups and Puppies*.

And you can also check out the first in R.L. Merrill's Crafty Tale Series, *A Peace Offering*:

Dover Billings has sold his handcrafted wares at the Dickens Fair in San Francisco for over twenty years. He's not as outgoing as the other artisans at this yearly Victorian celebration and prefers to observe the festivities from the shadows. That is until a new corset maker moves into the booth next door and unsettles his carefully constructed life. Landry Malcolm is handsome, well dressed, and the life of the party... one Dover wants no part of. Too bad he's attracted to his confident younger rival.

Landry desperately wishes to get through to the beautiful artist next door, but every move he makes seems to be the wrong one, until a drunken kiss breaks through Dover's serious demeanor. Miscommunications plague any attempts to find common ground, though, leaving Landry wondering what—if anything—he can do to make things right. Will a custom-made peace offering open the door to friendship, cooperation... and maybe more?

Other Holiday Tales from R.L. Merrill:

Father F'in' Christmas: A Minded Story (MF Paranormal Romance)

Love and Pride: Bolder Breed Studios (FF Contemporary Romance)

About Ro

Whether she's writing contemporary romance featuring quirky and relatable characters or diving deep into the paranormal and supernatural to give readers a shiver, R.L. Merrill loves creating compelling, diverse, and inclusive stories that will stay with readers long after. Winner of the Kathryn Hayes "When Sparks Fly" Best Contemporary award for *Hurricane Reese*, Paranormal Romance Guild's Best Rockstar Romance for *You Can Do Magic*, and Daphne DuMaurier finalist for *Connection*, Ro spends every spare moment improving her writing craft and striving to find that perfect balance between real-life and happily ever after. You can find her connecting with readers on social media, advocating for America's youth, cruising around town with Great Dane Velma, cuddling with twin black cat familiars Frankenstein and Dracula, or head-banging at a rock show near her home in the San Francisco Bay Area! ***Stay Tuned for more...***

Newsletter: www.rlmerrillauthor.com/all-the-links

ALSO BY R.L. MERRILL

Haunted Series: (Contemporary Romance)

Haunted

Fated

Bated

Jaded – (Coming Soon)

Minded Series: (Paranormal Spinoff of Haunted Series)

Minded

Blossomed

Father F'in' Christmas

A Peculiar Prom Night

Magic and Mayhem Universe: (Funny Paranormal Romance in the universe created by Robyn Peterman)

Shifted

Ghoul Me Once

Gator Me Twice

Magic and Mayhem/Shifted Collection

Fang Me Three Times

Fangtastic Four

Five Fanger Witch Punch

Hollywood Rock 'n' Romance Trilogy: (Contemporary Romance)

Teacher

Teacher: Act Two

Teacher: The Final Act

Contemporary Romance Series:

The Rock Season

Road Trip

You Fell First

The Heart Knows (Re-Releasing Soon)

A Match Made in Spain

LGBTQ Romance

Pinups and Puppies (Originally in Love Is All Vol. 2)

I Want, More – Bolder Breed Studios #1 (Originally in Love Is All Vol. 3)

Love and Pride – Bolder Breed Studios #2 (Originally in Love Is All Vol. 4)

Everything's Better With You: An MM Sports Romance

All I Wanna Do — Bolder Breed Studios #3 (Email Ro for your copy)

Under His Sheets: Accidentally Undercover – Out April 9, 2024

Feuds and Interludes: Road To Rocktoberfest 2024 - November 2024

The Banes of Lake's Crossing (Historical Horror Romance)

The Fourth Man (The Banes of Lake's Crossing) (Historical Horror Romance)

The Redemption of Nathaniel Bane

The Absolution of Jonah Bane

The Gifted Series: (Supernatural Suspense/Paranormal Romance)

Healer

Connection

<u>Protector</u>

Sundowners (M/M Paranormal Romance

<u>Sundowners Book One</u>

Sundowners Book Two (February 13, 2025)

Forces of Nature Series: (Gay Contemporary Romance)

Hurricane Reese

Typhoon Toby

<u>Earthquake Ethan</u>

Summer of Hush Series: (Gay Contemporary Romance)

Summer of Hush

Brains and Brawn

<u>You Can Do Magic: Carnival Of Mysteries (A Summer of Hush Tie-In</u>)

You Can Save Me: Carnival of Mysteries (Season Two, Book Two)

Anthologies:

Thanksgiving Day Parade From Hell (Worst Holiday Ever) (Gay Contemporary Romance

Valentine's Day From Hell (Worst Valentine's Day Ever) (Gay Contemporary Romance)

Salty and Sweet (Summer Fair) (Lesbian Contemporary Romance)

The Fourth Man (The Banes of Lake's Crossing) (Historical Horror Romance)

A Piece of Him (Gone With The Dead) (Horror)

<u>Breaking Bread</u>—Dark Divinations from HorrorAddicts.net Press (Horror)

Exchange (Renewal) (Science Fiction)

Tap-Tap-Tap (Impact) (Horror)

Human Sacrifice (Innovation) (Horror)

The Sitter (Clarity) (Horror)

Joy Is A Phone Call Away – A More Perfect Union (Lesbian Contemporary Romance)

The House Must Fall – Haunts and Hellions from HorrorAddicts.net Press – May 2021 (Horror)

A Kept Woman – BAQWA Presents: Horror Show 2021(Lesbian Horror Romance)

Gods of Rock 'n' Roll (Free on Wattpad)

How Bittersweet is Karma? Free on Wattpad)

Let Me Stand Next To Your Fire (Queer Cheer)

Midnight in the Renaissance Elevator

Holiday Romance

A Peace Offering (Re-release)

Love and Pride – Bolder Breed Studios #2

Once Upon A Holiday Story 2024 (Coming Soon)

Audiobooks

The Rock Season (Kiss App)

Brains and Brawn (Kiss App)

Teacher (Kiss App)

Hurricane Reese (Kiss App)

A Match Made in Spain (Audible)

Healer: Gifted Book One (Audible)

You Can Do Magic: Carnival of Mysteries (Audible)

Road Trip: A Rock 'n' Romance Story

Under His Sheets (Audible Coming Soon)

Non-Fiction

Horror Addicts Guide To Life Volume 2 - Edited by Emerian Rich

Death's Garden Revisited - Edited by Loren Rhoads (Out Fall 2022)